James

SAMUEL'S PRIDE SERIES BOOK 2

KATHI S. BARTON

This is a work of fiction. Names, characters, places, and incidents are products of the author's imagination or are used fictitiously and are not to be construed as real. Any resemblance to actual events, locations, organizations, or person, living or dead, is entirely coincidental.

WCP

World Castle Publishing, LLC
Pensacola, Florida

Copyright © Kathi S. Barton 2014
ISBN: 9781629890623
First Edition World Castle Publishing, LLC January 26, 2014
http://www.worldcastlepublishing.com

Cover: Karen Fuller
Editor: Eric Johnston

Dedication

To the real Valda LaRue! Thanks so much for the use of your name. It was perfect and I hope you enjoy your character. Sorry there are no Elvis' in here but hopefully Valda's evilness will make up for it. Thank you again, your newest fan, Kathi S. Barton

Chapter 1

Gab moved along the bodies one by one. She had her sheet of pictures, of course, but sometimes another vampire would sneak in and she'd take him out as well. When she happened upon a face that looked familiar, she paused. Something about him said to her "kill him." But there just wasn't enough information to cause her to take out the silver coins. Moving on, she thought of her job.

Right now she was a hunter, a hired killer. But when she finished here, taking out the vampires version of *most wanted*, she was going to have to go back to the one that paid the bills. And that was in the business of fixing up cars. Being a garage owner had its perks, and being able to do this when she wanted to was just one of many.

When she finished putting the coins on the bodies, she moved back toward the door. The man standing there startled her.

"You've been killing us," he accused. She nodded. There was no sense in denying what she'd been doing. Hell, she'd take out an ad in the paper if she wasn't afraid it would mess up her hunting ability. "That's not very sporting of you."

"Really? And here I thought it was damned nice of me." She frowned at him in a mocking way. "Oh, you mean to you? Well, sorry, but then I'm not out to make your life any better, now am I?"

"I'm going to enjoy killing you." She snorted at him. "You don't think I will? You're nothing but an arrogant human if you think that I cannot take you out."

"I've no doubt you're going to try. And you might even be able to hurt me a lot, but I'm still going to kill you. Your kind has been fucking up the world long enough." She raised her hands when he took a step toward her. "I'm only going to warn you once before I tell you that fucking with me is not going to make you happy. It might me, a great deal as a matter of fact but you'll still be dead."

"I think fucking you will make me very happy." His voice curled around her body like he'd meant for it to do, she was sure, but she only hardened her resolve and let the blades at her wrist slide forward. The sooner she got this over with, the better.

He leapt at her quickly, but Gab had had enough fights with vampires to know that they would and could move before she could see them. Instead of hitting her like she'd thought he intended, he slammed her against the wall with his power. The long blade in her right hand skittered to the floor from the impact and out of her reach. When he came at her the second time, she was prepared and swung out her fist and felt it connect with his mouth. Blood sprayed her face and she laughed at his apparent shock.

"You bitch." He spit out more blood and glared at her as the wound healed almost immediately. She hated that about vampires, their ability to heal before she could. "And here I was going to play with you. Now? Now you're going to simply die."

He came at her again, this time swiping at her body in a low arch. She felt the tear in her skin seconds before she sliced out with her blade. It made contact with him as she finished her move. She knew because he screamed as the silver tore into his body. Then he slashed out at her with his claw and knew that he'd cut her again. Gab felt the pain of being ripped open but couldn't stop to look. Her side, she knew, was going to need some major work to be put back together if she lived through this.

Blood loss was making her light-headed, so she jumped at him instead of backing off when he came at her again. She'd learned long ago by playing video games that it was better to move forward than retreat when something was coming at you. It sort of took the punch out of their swing and she could usually get a hit or two in on her own. When her blade entered his body, he dug his long, sharp claws into her shoulder, and it was all she could do to hang on to consciousness. The blood loss and the pain was making it hard to stay focused.

"You'll pay for this, bitch." She heard his hiss of breath as it left his body. Gab had to move quickly now and rammed the blade upward into his chest further. Gab knew the exact moment when it entered his heart. He knew it too apparently because the look on his face told her that she'd surprised him by killing him.

"Yeah, maybe. But you'll not be the one collecting." The vampire's hot breath moved over her cheek just as he turned to ash. There were screams behind her, plaintive screams that had her wishing she had plugs. The noise from their fight more than likely waking the vampires before the coins had a chance to work. But she didn't care. If they chased her now, they'd be just as dead. The sun was still shining in the sky and she was getting the fuck out of here now.

Gab walked into the sun feeling the heat of it almost immediately. She walked, or more likely staggered, to her truck and slid under the wheel. Looking down at the wound in her side, she cringed. This one was going to take her a while to heal from. Driving carefully, she made her way back to her small house.

Once there she sat in her truck for several minutes, waiting for the dizziness to pass. She looked down, her blood had soaked through her clothes and now pooled on the seat—this wasn't good. Moving gingerly out of the truck, she made her way into the house. Once again she was thankful, as she was every time she had to come home beat to shit that she'd opted for the house way off the beaten path. Once in the kitchen, she peeled off her clothes and dumped them into the trashcan as she moved by it. Cleaning up was the first thing on her list of things to do.

The shower water was stained a bright pink as it made its way down her body and to the drain. Blood poured profusely from all her wounds, but the one at her side was the most painful. Washing as much of the blood away as she could, she could see that the wound in her side needed stitches and turned off the water after she'd cleaned it as best she could. It was time to try and put herself back together again. As soon as the water stopped running over the larger wound, she knew it was going to be hard to close. The sucker just wouldn't stop bleeding.

It took her nearly three hours to get the stitches put in her side. Another hour or so to stitch up the others. Putting herself back together this time wasn't the worst she'd ever done, but it was ranking right up there around the top five. Taking some pain meds, she moved to her living room to sit on the couch and let them do their magic.

Going to bed would have been a waste of her time and the energy spent getting there would have been too much. With the amount of pain she was in, she knew that going to bed would have her tossing and turning and that too would hurt. Instead, she opted for watching old reruns and eating some day-old pizza that was on the table near her. Some things, she soon realized, were better left to be had only hot. The pizza didn't settle as well as she'd hoped or it was the drugs. The pain from her throwing up had her sweating bullets and cursing the fucking vamp again. After brushing her teeth twice she made her way back to the couch.

Settling down, she pulled her laptop to her, answered the email from her dad and mom, and tried to concentrate on what was going on with the show she was watching. Nothing was working, so she leaned back on the couch and thought about her day. She'd had a very productive one if she really thought of it.

Three oil changes earlier today, along with selling a set of tires to someone, wasn't the highlight, but it did pay some of her bills. For that she was happy.

There was the body work she'd been doing for a client. He had the same passion as she did for old cars, as well as restoring them, and she liked talking to him when he came around. She'd gotten the fender almost perfect, and now all she had to do was put it back on the car so it could be painted. Then just after midnight she'd gone on a hunt. After finding the nest she waited until they were all inside at nearly sunrise then entered. Along with three vampires that had been draining a younger woman she had gotten almost everyone on her list.

There had been ten photos on the sheet she'd been given for this job, and she got all but three. The man that had hurt her had been extra of course, and Gab hoped he'd asked her why she'd killed him too. She didn't know him well, but he could be a real pain in the ass about stupid shit when it suited him. She just might show him her wounds this time. Closing her eyes, she tried to think of anything but the pain.

Gab had been collecting silver coins all her life. It wasn't until her brother had died that she'd found a good use for them. Not that she generally didn't get them back she thought. But she had enough to use for some time if she didn't. Silva, the man she worked for always made sure she got them back and that they were clean of anything that might have come off the vampires. She'd discovered quite by accident that the coins were the quietest way to kill a vamp.

Initially she'd use a stake like they did in the movies. But she could only kill one or two before the nest would wake and find her. That had been stupid and dangerous.

Once when a vamp had taken exception to what she'd been about to do to him, she'd reached into her pocket and tossed the change at him. She noticed almost immediately that he backed off, and the skin where the silver ones touched burned deep. Yeah, it had been a really stupid idea at the time, but she'd been cornered and terrified. Now she used them most of the time.

To make her job easier and much safer, she simply laid a silver coin over his or her eyes and moved to the next picture on her list of vamps to take out. If she had enough time, she would put one in their mouth to keep them from screaming. She could do about a dozen before the first one would realize he'd been poisoned. Plenty of time for her to get out of the nest and well on her way. The silver would melt through their skin quickly, and once it got to their brain, they were dead. It was the same as having their heads lopped off. No brain, no body function. Then a few days later, Silva would give her the coins back and another sheet of pictures. Gab wondered if he'd give her a few days before he gave her another list this time. He never asked if she was hurt and she never told him how badly she was if she needed extra time.

The alarm going off startled her suddenly awake. Gab hadn't even realized she'd fallen asleep if she hadn't simply passed out and started to get up to shower. The pain coursing through her body had her seeing stars, and she moved a good deal slower to get dressed. Another perk of owning her own shop was that if she wanted to, she could take a few days off, which she decided to do. Then she remembered that she had to let the guy in to pick up his car to have it painted, and got dressed to go in.

"Fucking bastard." She cursed the vamp again and again as she tried to pull on her shoes without screaming. Settling on some boots that were as old as she was, she made her way to the truck, only to have to go back in the house to get a few rags. The blood from last night had soaked deep into the seats, but still remained wet enough to soak her if she sat on it. Tossing the rags over the stain, she slid into the truck made her way into Gab's Lube Job.

~~~

Jimmy wasn't thrilled about having to take the car in for repairs. He'd been in the middle of a nice argument with Kaleb when Kennedy had come into the room. She'd been complaining about the noise the car had been making for days now and asked him to take it in to have it looked at. Jimmy would do just about anything for the lioness, and this was no exception. She was his best friend's mate, and the two of them had been very good to him.

The truck out front of Gab's was blocking one of the bays and he had to drive by the garage and come back at the other angle. He pulled up near the only door and let the old car run in the event the garage was closed. Then he saw the man inside and wondered what was so funny. Even from where he was, outside the building he could hear the guy's laughter. The guy was dressed in a suit and laughing as if the guy standing next to him had told the best joke. Smiling, Jimmy went inside the doorway, only to find that the guy telling the joke wasn't a guy but a woman. And she was gorgeous.

"We're not really open today. If you want to leave your vehicle here, that's okay. We can get to it in a few days. Otherwise, you'll have to come back." Jimmy glanced at the man who had moved closer to the woman as she spoke. For some reason, Jimmy thought that he was protecting her. "We should be open again on Monday."

He had no idea why it bothered him that the man was there and she was telling him to go away, but he moved more into the bay where they were all standing. "It's making an odd noise and my…boss is going to have a baby. I think her husband just wants to make sure that it's nothing that'll get them hurt."

The woman looked at the man and then back at him, as if getting permission. When she nodded and moved toward the back of the bay, Jimmy went outside again. When the bay that hadn't been parked in front of opened he drove the car around and waited. She told him to pull it in slowly. Jimmy looked hard at the man who was still hovering over her and sent him a hard warning. Jimmy still wasn't sure why he cared but he did. The girl was probably this guy's kid or something.

By the time he was finished pulling in the car, the other man had left for which Jimmy was thrilled to see. The Camaro that had been in the bay they'd been standing near was now being covered up and he wondered briefly who it belonged to. Jimmy got out of the car after she told him to pop the hood.

"It's the transmission." Jimmy watched as she leaned into the engine area. "It sounds like it's shot. Probably needs to be overhauled."

"You can tell that by just looking?" She nodded, then shook her head. He started to ask her what she meant when she explained.

"Been doing this for a while, and I know the sounds it makes. I can overhaul it for your boss if she wants, but it'll be expensive. I'd say replace this car if they can afford it. A car this old is going to need parts that I'll have to pay shit tons for, if I can even find them." She moved to the office and Jimmy followed her. There was something about her that made him want to protect her. Jimmy leaned against the wall. She sat at the desk for about half a second, and then stood up with a groan. She moved into the bays and he followed her.

"So, what are you?" He wasn't sure why he'd asked her that, and expected her to tell him to get the fuck out of the garage, but she simply stopped for a second before walking to the car in the other bay, the one furthest away from him.

"A mechanic." She stared at him, and Jimmy had the overwhelming urge to squirm. He'd not felt this way around a woman since he'd been a pup in grade school.

"What else?" She had no scent. That alone made his wolf stir with caution. The woman simply had to be something more than just a mechanic. And his wolf wanted answers as badly as he did.

She shook her head and went back to leaning in the car. "I pump gas when I have to. Sometimes I'll even sweep the floor. And if the day hasn't been a total loss like this one has been so far, I can go home with more money than I came in with. Why?"

"Are you a human?" She paused and glanced his way again without moving from the car. Jimmy started to stand from the wall he'd been leaning against when she turned to him. She didn't look amused.

"Are you?" He shook his head. She watched him, and this time he did shift on his feet. "I see. But you're not vampire because the sun is out, so you must be something else. Not that I care, mind you. You haven't done anything that makes me have to kill you, yet anyway. You're going to be fine so long as you keep it that way."

As she turned back to the car, he leaned back against the wall. He wished she didn't smell so powerfully of gasoline and grease. A scent of something sweet came from her occasionally that would make his beast growl when he got a whiff of it, but he didn't have a clue as to why. She wasn't even dressed like a woman. Her clothes were ill-fitting and dirty.

When she spoke again, he stood there for several seconds before he asked her to repeat herself. He'd been so wrapped up in what she was dressed like he'd missed it.

"I said your car can stay here until Thursday. But just call me if they decided to scrap this one. I might be on a job, and I'd hate for you to waste your time."

He'd been dismissed. It might have been funny, but he did leave her alone for now. He'd have to have someone find out about her and this place before he came back though. And he would, if for no other reason than to see what he could find out about her. There was something so…he wasn't sure but there was something.

Jimmy was moving toward the woods just behind the garage when he heard a gunshot. Pausing he looked around to see if he could see anyone, but he just knew it was the girl and that she was in trouble. She'd either been playing with a gun and it went off or someone was robbing her. Either way, he had to save her ass.

As he ran into the building then into the bay she'd been in, he nearly fell. There was blood everywhere. Jimmy started to call out for her, and that's when he realized he didn't know her name and for some reason he didn't think she looked all that much like a Gab. Jimmy started to reach for Samuel when he saw a pair of feet lying just in front of the car he'd brought in. Slowly, he moved closer to see who it was and knew immediately the man was half human and half vampire.

Jimmy also knew he was dead without having to check his pulse. The neat hole in his forehead said it all. He heard her speaking and moved toward the sound being as quiet as he could. Jimmy realized she was talking to someone, but he couldn't see who. Then she cried out in pain and Jimmy told Samuel to get his ass there.

"She's in trouble. I have to see to her." Samuel told him to be careful and that he was on his way. *"There's a vamp here too. Dead. You might want to tell Stephan."*

Jimmy didn't remember moving, but he was in the room when she cried out again. The large man that held her had blood on his shirt as well as his face. Jimmy wondered what the fuck had happened in the two minutes he'd been gone.

"Let her go." The man laughed at him. "I don't want to have to kill you, but—"

"She ain't gonna hunt us no more." Jimmy thought about pointing out the double negative, but doubted the man would understand the humor. Especially since he'd just claimed she was indeed going to hunt again. Then it occurred to him what he'd said.

"Hunt you? What? You work for the police?" She rolled her eyes, and he frowned. She certainly didn't look like she could be someone who repo-ed cars, but how the hell was he supposed to know. And he was sure it was a good deal more than what he thought this half breed vamp was talking about.

"Not exactly." She groaned when the big man jerked her hair. "Why don't you run along? I'm sort of in the middle of something right now and you're fucking up my ability to finish it. If you go now, I'll tell your boss that I'll look extra hard for those parts for her car."

Jimmy crossed his arms over his chest. She could not be serious. She was telling him to get the hell out and to leave her alone with this asshole. She was fucking nuts.

"You want me to go away?" She nodded even as the rogue yanked her head back more. "And what will you do? Fight him off, then finish with the transmission on the car?"

"It's an oil change if you must know, but yeah, I suppose so. But I really hoped you'd be out of here. I sort of work—"

"What the hell are you two going on about? In case you didn't see this, I've got me the bitch right where I want her." The man jabbed the knife into her throat and blood poured from the small wound. Jimmy hadn't even seen the knife until then. "She and I have some serious business to conduct. And you'll have to wait your turn."

Before Jimmy could say anything about the moron's comment, he was gone. Not gone but dead gone, a silver blade still quivering in his chest. The woman was standing there with another silver blade in her hand and her back to him. Christ, had she really moved that fast?

"You killed him." She laughed a short bark of laughter. Then she turned to him slowly. "Christ, you're hurt."

Blood poured from her shoulder and waist. He wasn't sure why, but he didn't think the dead men had done it to her but it had happened before they had arrived. She seemed to favor her left leg too when she moved toward him. Jimmy could tell she wasn't any happier with him than the dead man had been with her.

Jimmy took a step toward her and then one back. He was taking another back when he hit the counter behind him. She stopped advancing on him as well.

"I was hurt yesterday. Or the day before, I can't remember." She staggered to the desk and leaned heavily on it. "I'd very much like it if you left now. I've got a lot of shit to do today."

Jimmy didn't point out that all she was going to do today was bleed to death. But he had a feeling she knew that. As she sat down, he moved toward her. Right now her safety seemed much more important than the blade she still held in her hand. Jimmy knelt down in front of her and put his hand on her wrist.

"Your pulse is slowing." She nodded and rolled her eyes. "I want you to know that there is help on the way. And that you'll be in good hands when they arrive."

"I don't need any help." Her voice was low now, and he had to listen hard to hear her. His hearing was excellent, but she was fading fast. "There's another man in the bay. I killed him as well."

Jimmy nodded. She went limp, and he started to pick her up when she opened her eyes and stared at him. He had a feeling she had no idea he was still there. When she focused on his face she smiled slightly before speaking again.

"There's this man named Silva. I don't remember his first name. He's a vamp too. A pain in my ass, but then all of them are hungry pricks only out for themselves. Tell him I didn't just kill these two. It was self-defense." She closed her eyes again. "I don't know how to contact him."

"I know him." She nodded, and this time when she started to slide out of the chair, he picked her up and laid her on the floor. He was tearing open her tee-shirt when the door to the office crashed open. Stephan Silva stood there looking like an avenging angel.

"She's been hurt." Stephan nodded and moved toward them, and Jimmy felt his wolf growl low. Stephan stopped. "I don't know why I did that, but please stay back unless you plan to help her."

"I'll help her if you'll allow it. I can't be here long, but long enough to give her enough blood to survive. It's all I'm able to do for her." Jimmy had a moment to think on that. So the two of them had an arrangement. Then Stephan was leaning over the girl and tore open his wrist, but instead of giving it to her to drink from, he only dropped a few droplets into her mouth.

"I don't suppose you know what happened to her." Stephan only stared at him as he licked his wounds closed. "I guess that's a no. She told me to tell you that she didn't have a choice in killing these two. I suppose if I asked you about that I'd get nothing either."

"She works for me. Not that she's happy about it, but she does it anyway. Other than that," Stephan shrugged. "You'll have to ask her. And don't be surprised if she tells you to fuck off. She tells me often enough."

Samuel arrived when the medics did. She was being transported to the clinic and not the regular hospital for which Jimmy was grateful to find out. Stephan said he'd pay all her bills, but he wanted her to have the best and there, he knew, she'd get it. She was still out when they closed the doors to the ambulance.

"Her name. What is it?" Stephan looked at the shop behind him as they stood in the parking lot. "You're not going to tell me she's Gab, are you?"

"She is. Gabriel Parker. According to her, there was a mix-up at the hospital and her name was changed when put on her birth certificate. I think someone just had a good sense of humor." Stephan smiled at him as he continued. "What is she to you? Mate?"

"Christ, no. I just brought Kennedy's car in to be looked at. Nothing more. I just happened to be here when this shit went down." Stephan nodded and moved away. When he disappeared, Jimmy looked around for a way to get to the clinic to see to her. Not that he knew what he could do but still he wanted to make sure she was getting cared for. Samuel offered him a ride to the hospital, then he'd take him home. Jimmy decided it would be better than walking and hopped into his car to follow the ambulance out.

Chapter 2

Wiley watched his daughter sleep. She'd not moved in over three hours and he was concerned. Actually, he was terrified, but he was trying his best to be brave for his wife. Janice wasn't taking this as well as he was. He looked over at her now.

"She'll be fine." Janice nodded once and kissed Gab's hand before laying it on the bed again. She'd been doing that since they'd arrived two days ago. "The nice doctor told us that she had lost a great deal of blood and that—"

"I was standing right next to you, Wiley. I heard every word that nice man said. What I didn't know and still don't is how she managed to get so injured when we were promised that she'd be fine doing what she's doing. How does one get so hurt working as a mechanic?" He didn't answer her because, frankly, the same questions had been going through his mind as well. Wiley was afraid he knew the answer as well as his wife did.

"She'll tell us as soon as she wakes up. It's probably nothing more than something hit her while she was working on an engine." Janice glared at him, and he decided to brave the truth with her. "I think she's doing something on the side and that she's doing it because of Rusty."

Janice nodded and picked up Gab's hand again. This time when she kissed it, she held it to her cheek. When she finally looked at him, Wiley could see that she thought the same thing.

"I knew that she'd not be able to leave this alone about Rusty. She was more hurt than we'd all thought her to be. She probably blames herself." Wiley nodded. He thought his daughter also knew more than she'd told them…a great deal more.

"His death was hard on all of us, but her finding him…her seeing him leap? That was just too much for any of us. Especially her." Wiley had his doubts about the way Rusty had killed himself as well, but didn't speak of it. They had enough going on right now. Instead, he asked her about the doctor. "Did you know that the doctor that is caring for her is recently married? I was talking to him this morning and he said that he and his wife were expecting their first child."

Wiley looked at his little girl and wondered if she'd ever settle down. He didn't think she would any time soon, but he still dreamed of having grandchildren to hold and play with. Smiling, he thought of all the fun at Christmas they'd have spoiling them. Wiley glanced at Janice when he felt her staring at him. That woman could read him like a book.

"You get those thoughts right out of your head right now." He started to ask her what she meant when she answered his unspoken question. "She's not going to be having any children if anyone finds out she's got a doctorate in Behavioral Science and owns a garage. Men will think she's nuts."

"They more than likely do already." They both stood when Gab spoke. She licked her lips three times before she attempted to speak again. "What are you doing here anyway? I thought you were going on that cruise?"

"We went last month, darling. I sent you all those nice pictures from our cell phone." Gab nodded at her mom. "We came as soon as that nice doctor called us."

"What doctor?" When she looked at him she looked panicky, and he found that he wanted to grab for his gun. It had been years since he'd done that, and wanting to do so now scared him not just a little. "How did I get here?"

"Doctor Murray. He said you'd been his patient before." When Gab sat up, he could almost hear her pain. Her face contorted three times before she let out her breath. "Baby, I don't think you're well enough to get up yet."

"I have to go. I have to get home. I have stuff to....What did this Murray guy look like?" He nodded as Janice answered her.

"Tall, dark haired, and very handsome. I think he's on call right now because he told us he'd be back later this evening. The poor man said he'd been on call all night." Gab moved to the edge of the bed just as the door behind Wiley opened. When Gab snarled, it was everything Wiley could do not to cringe from her. The doctor seemed to think she was funny for some reason.

"I told you to stay out of my life. That was our deal. You give me what I need and I do the job. Nothing else." The doctor took her wrist, and Gab jerked it from him. "What are you telling my parents?"

"Nothing. And our deal was I help you stay alive. I did. You were dying when I got there." She looked at him as the doctor continued. "It's a horrible thing to get hurt on the job as you did, but even worse when you don't tell your boss when you're hurt."

"Gab?" Wiley took a step toward his daughter when she laid back. He knew she was hurting when tears started to flow down her cheeks. He hated to see her cry more than he did anyone. A nurse came in and gave her a shot in her IV. Gab didn't protest at all, and that worried him more than anything.

"I want to be alone." Janice started to protest, but Gab held up her hand. "I have to talk to the two of you later, but right now I have to speak to him."

They both looked at the doctor. The man looked like he could take on the world, and Wiley had a feeling that when they stepped out of the room, he might be better off doing just that. Gab looked mad enough to murder.

As they stepped into the hall, the nice young man from the other day came toward them. He took them both down the hall and sat with them when Janice told him that the doctor was in there with their daughter. Wiley watched the young man, wondering what his connection with Gab was. Jimmy Burger for some reason didn't look like he was any happier with Gab than she was with the doctor. Wiley was almost afraid to find out what she wanted to tell them.

~~~

"I didn't mean to kill those men. Well, I did, but they left me no choice. It was me or them and as much as I know you'd wish it was me, it's not." Stephan huffed at her as she continued. "And there was a witness. You'll have to debrief him."

"Jimmy won't tell anyone. He's a wolf, did you know that?" She nodded, and Stephan raised a brow. "He told you what he was or you knew?"

"I didn't know what he was, but he said he wasn't human. He asked me what I was. There was some confusion as to whether or not I'm human." Stephan knew that while she did have some of his blood in her system, she was full human.

"And what did he say to that?" Jimmy had already told him about their conversation, and not that he didn't believe the young pup, but he did want to hear what she thought of the younger man. Stephan thought there was something about the two of them, but didn't comment on it just yet.

"Nothing. I think maybe I passed out and the rest you probably know more than me." She shifted on the bed and he waited. Something that Stephan had a great deal of was patience. Though this girl above all others tested it at times, he still waited for her. "There was another man. The one that did this to me. I killed him as well."

"Do you know who he was? And for the record, you can kill those that try to kill you first. I know that you expect me to be pissed at you for taking out a rogue that wasn't on your list, but I'd much prefer you being alive than them." She didn't answer, and he knew she wouldn't. He'd been telling her this since she'd come to him all those months ago. He thought about that while watching her fight sleep. The meds that they'd given her were finally kicking in.

She'd been walking the streets late one night. The weather had turned unseasonably cold, yet she was only dressed in a pair of dark jeans and tee-shirt. He could smell the silver on her from his hiding spot not ten feet from her. When another vamp started toward her, he growled low and took off. When another came toward her thirty minutes later, Stephan had decided to see what she was about.

It was over almost as soon as it started. The vampire, younger than the girl, had overpowered her almost immediately. But she'd fought with all she was worth and then some. Still, she had no skill and not a lick of sense as far as he could tell. When he killed the vamp before he tore her throat out, he was tempted to taste her himself when he got a good look at her.

Dark hair pulled back into a sloppy ponytail hung down her back. She had darker eyes than he'd ever seen on a human, and skin so creamy that he'd bet that milk would pale in comparison. Full lips and a fuller body made his beast want to press her against the wall behind her and take her and all she had to offer. And for some reason, that pissed him off. Grabbing her by the throat, he did press her against the wall, but not the way he'd wanted.

"What the fuck is wrong with you? Are you trying to become a meal for just about any vampire that comes along? Do you have any idea what would have happened to you—?"

She kicked him in the groin, and he dropped her. She came at him twice more before he was able to subdue her.

25

And in those few minutes he'd had to fight hard not to end up as dead as the other vamp. She wasn't just fighting. She was in a killing rage.

"Stop." She knocked away his compulsion as easily as he'd done so with her knife. He grabbed her around the waist, pinning her arms to her, and held her tightly. When her struggles began to slow, he started to talk to her. "You're here to kill any vampire, or is there one in particular you're gunning for?"

"I already got the one I wanted. Now I'm going to rid the earth of you all." She renewed her struggles, but he simply squeezed her tighter until she settled. Stephan told her he'd let her go if she'd stop trying to kill him.

"I would like to hire you." She turned and looked at him over her shoulder. "You have some passable skills as a hunter, but not enough to keep you from getting drained. First of all, we can smell your silver, so we tend to avoid that if possible."

"The other guy didn't." Stephan nodded. "So just some of you can smell it and not all. That's not what I was told."

"By who? Never mind, it doesn't matter. We can all smell it. All supernaturals can. But he was hungry, and he thought to overpower you before you got a chance to use it on him." She asked to be let go. "You'll simply talk to me then?"

"Yes. I don't know why you're telling me this. Or not killing me, but I'll listen until you start boring me." For all her bravado he did like her. She was prickly and sometimes a bitch, but she'd listened to him that night and for the next month when he'd trained her. Fat lot of good it had done them when her first night out she'd nearly gotten killed. He'd been much more careful of where he'd sent her since. When the door opened behind him, he started to draw the shadows around him to protect her, but stopped when he saw it was Jimmy.

"She's going to be all right?" Stephan nodded at Jimmy. "Samuel sent me in to check on her. I was going into town anyway and told him I would."

Stephan had talked to Samuel not an hour ago so he knew that the young pup was lying. Stephan watched him walk to the bed and look down on the girl. That's when he knew that what he'd thought was happening was true. This was Jimmy's mate. And he knew that neither of them were going to be happy about it.

"I've taken away her scent." Jimmy looked at him when Stephan spoke. "She works for me and has been hunting for me for several months. She told me that she was injured by someone who wasn't on her list of most wanted."

"You have her working for you doing what exactly? Hunting for them and bringing them to you, or more?" Stephan didn't answer Jimmy, but he got it anyway. "She's a fucking human, and you have her hunting rogues and killing them for you? Are you fucking insane? She could get killed."

"I think that was her plan." Jimmy stared at him for several seconds before he sat down. "And she would be dead had I not taken her under my wing and trained her. Taking away her scent was all she's allow me to enhance her with."

Jimmy stared at the girl for several seconds, not speaking. Stephan knew the young man, and also knew that he seldom did anything without thinking about it over and over. The same with what he said. Whatever he was thinking was going to be a question that would give him the right answer without a lot of explanations.

"She means something to me. I haven't figured out what yet, but I'd just as soon her not be my mate." Jimmy looked at him then. "She's going to be, isn't she?"

"Would you like to smell her?" Jimmy stood up and started pacing instead of answering him. The man was ten kinds of pissed right now, so instead of poking at him he kept his mouth shut. He didn't feel like having to hurt the man.

"It'll make it no less true, will it?" Stephan told him it wouldn't. "I don't want to smell her. I want to stay away from her. And you'll keep this to yourself. If Kennedy gets wind of this, she'll make me...she'll try and make me take her. And I fucking don't want a mate. Now or ever."

"All right." Stephan wanted to take his hold off the girl and give Jimmy her scent, but he wouldn't do that. Not yet at any rate. He himself didn't want a mate either, and had taken precautions to never find one. There was no fucking way a woman was going to tie him up on knots again.

After Jimmy left, Stephan reached out to a few of his minions. They were told to watch the clinic at all costs. The sun was just cresting when he left Gab. On his way out he stopped by the lounge to see her parents. They were both sleeping on the couch, and he wondered if anyone had made them arrangements to stay somewhere. Stephan reached out to Samuel.

"We've offered to let them stay here, but they won't leave the hospital except to go to the hotel across the street. It's being taken care of as well. Which I guess I can understand. But we have made sure that they're fed every day and that anything they need is right there." Stephan thanked him. *"What is she to you? And don't give me some shit about her being your child or something. She's a human."*

"She works for me." He debated for all of ten seconds before he told him the rest. *"I've ordered some extra security around the clinic. She's a bit of a hothead, so I'd not mention this to her. Also, something else you should be aware of, she's a hunter. While she knows there are others, she isn't able to tell what is human or not."*

"I see." Samuel was quiet for several seconds. *"As a hunter I would imagine that's why she's hurt in the first place. Anything else I should know?"*

Stephan told him plenty. *"But for now you will just have to wait. I've some things I have to do before I rest for the day, and one of them is to find out who hurt her. I have an idea but nothing solid as yet. Also, she has no scent. I've worked a little of my magic and taken it from her for reasons I'm sure you can guess."*

"All right. You do know that instead of answering any of the million or so questions that are rumbling around in my head you're making more, right?" Samuel laughed before continuing. *"Jimmy has been asking about her too. I guess he feels a little responsible for her since he was there when she finally fell."*

"You should also know that he's her mate. Jimmy doesn't want Kennedy to know either because he's sure she'll make sure that he bonds with her." Stephan waited while Samuel laughed. He fought hard not to join him. Jimmy was going to be mated and bonded to this girl before the week was out, he just knew it.

"So, he doesn't want my mate to know. Oh, this is going to be fun. I'm not going to tell her, but I'm going to have all kinds of fun putting them together. Do you need him for anything? Like to watch over her?"

"I think he'd guess what I was doing, don't you? Perhaps you can take care of that on your end. But know this, if he hurts her before they mate, I'll kill him. The girl may not be my child, but I take care of what is mine." Samuel assured him he understood completely. *"Also another thing, her brother was a vampire. He died about eight months ago. I'm not at liberty to give you details as yet, but his name was Rusty Parker."*

"I'm writing it down now. I'm assuming there will be sufficient information on the Internet about him?" Stephan told him there was. *"But you think it's all a big lie."*

"It is a lie. The boy didn't kill himself, but I don't know for sure who did. The paper ran something to the effect that he killed himself. And I don't think her parents know. Or at

least that's what Gab says." Stephan looked at the couple that were just starting to wake up and wondered how much they really knew. *"I'm going to have the Parkers give you a call. They need to be somewhere safe, and sleeping here in the clinic isn't. Don't be surprised when you get the call."*

Stephan closed the connection after telling Samuel that he'd pay for the added expense of having the Parker's watched. Of course the lion had said no, but Stephan was going to make the arrangements all the same. He walked to the Parkers as they were standing.

"She's doing better, my girl?" He nodded at Mr. Parker. "Still don't know why we're here instead of a real hospital, but the other man said it was because this one was closer."

"It was, and this hospital is more specialized. She had some extensive wounds." Stephan had them follow him to the restaurant across the street. He knew that they needed to eat because he did as well. But not what was on the menu. "I think she's getting the best care here."

"She's all we have left." Stephan looked at Mrs. Parker and knew that she wasn't as naïve as she appeared. "We don't want anything to happen to her, but she insisted that she wanted to be a mechanic when she graduated from college. She seems to do very well at it."

Stephan nodded and took a breath before speaking. It was time to help the girl whether she wanted it or not. "She's mentioned her brother. What do you really know of his death?"

Mr. Parker looked away, and Mrs. Parker paled. They knew. Neither of them knew for sure, and he was positive that they'd never talked about it with each other, but they knew something was wrong. When Mrs. Parker spoke, he knew that they hadn't.

"He wrote me a letter before he...before he died." Mr. Parker looked at her, shocked. "I never told anyone because...well, frankly, I didn't want to believe it. He said some things that…Rusty wasn't a fanciful young man, but some of the things he told me were scary."

"He told you what he was." She nodded at him and took her husband's hand. "Did he tell you who did it to him?"

"No. All he said was that several weeks before he…before the letter, that he'd been converted. He told me that he was a monster and that he was going to end himself before he hurt anyone else. I was never sure what he meant by that, but after reading about vampires on the Internet I could well imagine what had happened. He had to eat someone, didn't he?"

"No. He would have had to feed from someone, but not eat them." Stephan looked at Mr. Parker. "You didn't know this, did you?"

"No. I knew that he'd been…something was off about him, but he'd never talk about it to me. He said…I don't want you to take this the wrong way because my boy was a good man. But he was closer to his mother than to me. Course he'd talk to her." He looked at his wife. "I just wish you'd have told me. I've been crazy with worry."

"You said you never wanted to talk about it." Mr. Parker nodded as his wife continued. "I wanted to talk to you. So badly. But you just…Rusty was so depressed. He called himself a monster and all sorts of things. He told me that the person who changed him said that he'd live forever, and that bothered him."

"How so?" Stephan watched as Mrs. Parker struggled with what he'd asked her. She looked at her husband before she answered.

"He said that outliving us was going to be hard on him anyway even if he was human, but to be a monster and know that he was going to be killing others to do so was more than he wanted to deal with." She looked at him then with the same hardness he'd seen in her daughter. "Rusty wasn't a coward. He was a good boy and a better man than anyone I know. He did this because someone forced him to. I know it."

"I believe you." And he did too. The suicide had never rang true with him. A newly formed vampire didn't meet the sun willingly. It wasn't something an old one did well either. But he knew that as soon as the pain would have started—and there would have been a great deal of it—anyone, especially a new convert, would have gone for cover, not stayed until they were ash. Someone had staked him to the ground, Stephan would bet anything. Or had removed his head.

"What are you?" Mrs. Parker flushed. "I'm sorry, but I no longer believe you're a doctor. I was a nurse for many years and you're not a doctor any more than I'm a man. So, what are you?"

"A vampire."

Chapter 3

Gab woke up to a bright room. She knew where she was now. A clinic on Tenth that she'd passed a million times on her way to the garage. What she didn't know was why she was there and not at a regular hospital.

"Are you hungry?" She looked at the nurse who'd been caring for her for days now. "I've been instructed to let you have whatever you'd like. And today the cook is Oran, and he is a fantastic cook."

"When can I be released?" Gab had asked the same question every time she woke over the past five days. And she never got an answer. So she wasn't surprised when the woman went on about breakfast choices as if she'd not spoken. And today, Gab had had enough.

Tossing back the covers, she was glad now that she'd looked at her body last night. Sleep was harder to come by now that she hadn't been exhausting herself into a coma, and she'd had nothing to occupy her time last night but thought. The nurse took a step toward her.

"You touch me and it'll be the last thing you ever do." Gab didn't feel bad when she paled. "I'm leaving here. I've had enough of this shit, and if you or anyone else tries to stop me, I'll kill you. Do you understand?"

"You're not going to get past security. They have guns." Gab reached under her pillow and pulled out the gun her father had brought her the third day and laid it across her lap.

She'd been surprised when he'd brought it in, and more so when he said he'd had it loaded with silver.

"You're not going to stop me, and neither are they." Gab stood up and held onto the gun and the bed. She was light-headed but didn't let it stop her from leaving. As soon as the nurse left her, Gab went to find her clothes. Her dad had been very helpful in helping her break out. Smiling, she turned when the door opened again. She wasn't going to be stopped.

"You think you'll need a ride home?" Gab looked at the man, confused as he sat down in the chair. She didn't know who he was, nor did she know why he was asking her. "I was in the neighborhood and Anna told me that you were leaving. I take it you're not waiting to see if you're released. I'm Samuel Payne by the way. I'm a friend of Stephan's."

"Where is he? I'd like to shoot him right about now." Samuel laughed and told her he didn't know. "Why are you helping me? And just so you know, being a friend of Stephan's isn't going to get you any brownie points."

"Yeah, he said you'd be pissed off. Actually, he said you'd still be pissed off. You and he, you have a strange relationship." Gab snorted. "Anyway, I was here for an appointment and heard that you were going to shoot the place up if you didn't get to leave. And as much as I hate hospitals, I own this one and would very much like for it to be a safe place for us to come when we need help. Where did you get the gun?"

She ignored his question with one of her own. "You're just going to let me leave? No trying to stop me or using any...what are you anyway?"

"Lion. You're a human and know a great deal about supernaturals, I understand." She shrugged. "Then you know that the silver you have in your gun will kill most of the beings here. So if you wouldn't mind, I'd very much appreciate it if you'd put that the fuck away."

"I don't think so. I've been beat to shit, knocked around, and generally treated like a punching bag for the past eight months. I have no reason to trust you, less now knowing that you're Stephan's friend, and I'm not going to be caught with my pants down again. But I will tell you this. I'm not going to shoot anyone that doesn't try to kill me first. It's the best you're going to get from me."

He watched her. She didn't move around or squirm but stood still. Men like him, large and too muscled for her tastes, scared the shit out of her, but she wasn't going to back down...not ever again. When the door opened again, she stared at the man who'd been in her garage the day she'd killed those two men. She watched as the big lion stood up and hugged him, and nearly whimpered when the newcomer walked toward her. There was something too...well, too everything about this man.

"I'm to take you to your home and make sure it's safe." She looked over his shoulder to Samuel when the other man spoke. "He's my boss of sorts, and he said I was to take care of you."

"I don't need a sitter." Samuel laughed at her. "I'm serious. You offered me that ride and while I appreciate it, I can find my own way home."

"Tough. You'll ride with him or I'll have you chained to the bed and held until I feel you're safe from the world." Gab started to argue with him when he suddenly looked more lion than man. "Don't fuck with me, Gabriel Parker. I'm much bigger and much meaner than you'll ever be."

Gab went to the bathroom without speaking to either of them. She'd just see about her getting out of this place. Once she had the door closed and locked, she pulled off her gown. Trying her best not to look at her side, she dressed as quickly as she could without hurting herself. Then when she was dressed, she pulled out her brush and pulled it once through her hair before she had to sit down. The knock on the door had her glaring at it.

"Are you okay? I heard you moan." She looked around the room to see if there was a speaker. There was no way he'd heard her tiny moan. "My hearing is exceptional. I can hear that your heart rate has increased in the past few moments, telling me that you're either aroused or pissed. I'm thinking pissed."

"Fuck off." His laughter told her that he'd heard her whisper. "You think this is funny? Well I don't. I just want you ass wipes to leave me the fuck alone."

"Too late for that." She didn't understand his statement but said nothing. Bringing the brush up again, she tried her best to get some of the tangles out of her hair, but it was too much. Right now she'd gladly crawl back into the bed and never wake. But getting home was a priority.

When she came out of the bathroom, he'd pulled her things from the tiny closet and had them lying on the bed. She didn't say anything to him but began stuffing them into the duffle that was lying there. He moved her out of the way and dumped them out, only to fold them up again and put them neatly in the duffle.

"Are you gay?" He looked at her, Then down her body. She caught fire just that quickly. "You're folding my laundry like an old woman."

"Perhaps I just wanted them neat and not wrinkled like you seem to prefer." When he zipped the duffle up and took a step toward her, she backed up. "You're very beautiful; are you aware of that?"

"No. I'm plain." She wasn't lying to him. She did think of herself as plain. When he had her pressed tightly against the wall and yet not touching her, she closed her eyes. Fear was overriding her need to look into his face. "Back the fuck up."

Her voice was husky. Not fearful like she felt, but as if she'd had her throat scorched by something. Images of his tongue in her mouth had her glancing at him as she licked her lips.

"You're not what I want." Before she could tell him she didn't fucking care, he brushed his mouth over hers softly. "And there is no way we're going to consummate this relationship."

"I don't know what you mean." His fingers curled into her hair as he tilted her head. Licking her lips again, she looked at his as they lowered to her mouth. Gab felt her mind turn to mush at the thought of him kissing her. "You should know that I don't want you to kiss me."

"You should know that I have no choice." His mouth took hers and she moaned. There was nothing gentle about his kiss, nothing soft and loving. It was to take and take again. His tongue invaded and conquered. His breath heated her flesh and branded her. Before she could touch him like he was her, she felt herself chill, his body no longer near her but across the room. He'd leapt away from her as if she had a disease.

"You're not going to be my mate. I don't want you." She nodded, not entirely sure what he was talking about. "I'll take you to your home, but I don't want anything to do with you. Ever. Do you understand me?"

It took her a few seconds before what he was saying to her registered. He'd said this to her as if she'd done the kissing, as if she'd been the one to press him against the wall. Before she said something really stupid like telling him she didn't care what he wanted, that she wanted him now, she went to the phone. When a nurse answered it, she spoke to her but looked at the man.

"I would like for you to call me a cab please. The person in here with me is not taking me home. And tell that big lion guy that if he makes me, I'll kill him and the prick in here." The nurse told her she'd see what she could do. "No you won't. You'll call a cab or so help me I will shoot this man."

When she put down the phone, the man walked toward her. She pointed the gun at him and he stopped. She wasn't in any mood to fuck with him. When the nurse came in a few minutes later to tell her that the cab was there, she looked between Gab and the man for several seconds. Then she laughed.

"I've contacted Samuel as well. I guess he was right." Gab didn't bother asking her about what, but the man did. "He said she was more than likely ready to kill your ass and that you'd fucked up. I guess I'll have to pay up. Never would have thought that the famous James Burger wouldn't be able to take on one small human."

~~~

Jimmy watched her cab pull away. He was so pissed off right now that if anyone said one thing to him he'd likely kill them. His beast wasn't very happy with him either. He wanted him to go and get her and bring her back, or better yet, take her to the woods and fuck her until he was satisfied. Jimmy was going to find Stephan and cut his throat out. He just knew the vamp had made it so he could smell her.

Making his way to his car, he felt Samuel touch his mind. The fucking nurse had probably already called him and now he was going to get a lecture. He wasn't in the mood for one either.

"So, you want to tell me why the woman you were set to watch is now going home alone? I gave you an order and I expect it to—"

"Then you should have ordered her to behave herself." Jimmy flushed when he realized what he'd said. *"I'm going there now to make sure she's okay. But we had a disagreement and she's pissed off. I've never met an angrier woman in my life."*

"What did you do to her?"

Jimmy started to tell Samuel that he'd done nothing to the crazy woman, but that would be a lie. He'd done all kinds of things to her. Tasting her was top on the list.

"You had to do something. She was willing to go with you when I left."

38

"I might have said something to her to upset her." Samuel laughed and Jimmy wanted to scream at him that it wasn't funny. *"She doesn't have a sense of humor."*

"I guess not. Or maybe you're not as funny as you think you are." Jimmy didn't think he was funny at all but said nothing. Samuel was on a roll and he didn't want to prolong this by pointing out that he'd ordered him to do something he'd told him only that morning he didn't want to do. *"She's important to Stephan. She works for him."*

Jimmy knew that but hadn't been aware that Samuel knew. Not that it was any of his business, but he wanted to know how much Samuel knew. *"She his house keeper or something?"*

"No. She hunts for him."

Jimmy stopped at the next light and let that statement settle. Hunter. So she really was a hunter and Stephan hadn't been pulling his leg.

"She can't do that. She's...." He'd started to say she was his mate and that he'd forbid it, but had a feeling that if Samuel didn't already know who she was to him, then saying that would bring Kennedy down on his ass. And she was an equal opportunity ass kicker. *"She's not well yet."*

"I think he's aware of that." Samuel laughed again. *"Are you going to make sure that she's healthy again? Or are you going to sulk because you think she should do what you tell her and not question what you say."*

He knew. Jimmy wasn't sure how he'd figured it out, but he knew that Gab was his mate. He'd bet his last buck that Stephan had told him. And if he knew, it was only a matter of time before Kennedy knew.

"I'm not going to have anything to do with her. And from now on I'd very much appreciate it if you didn't try and throw us together again. I'm assuming that's why I was told to take her home." Samuel laughed. *"This is not funny, you stupid cat."*

"But it is. And no, I didn't toss you two together. I was bringing Mom in for her physical therapy when I heard one of the nurses say she had a gun and it was loaded with silver. I thought it better that I didn't leave my mother behind at her appointment to take a girl home when you were right there as well. You're not going to take her as your mate, I take it?"

"Never." Jimmy was nearly to Gab's house when he thought of something else. *"Does Kennedy know?"*

For an answer Samuel started laughing. She knew as well, and Jimmy had a feeling that she was not going to forget this. He was going to be mated to this woman before the end of the week, he simply knew it.

The house was sitting far back from the road and surrounded by trees. The woods behind the house and on either side were beautiful this time of year with their fall colors, and he could see himself running through them with a few of his friends. He tried not to think about running with Gab. First, she wasn't a wolf, and secondly, he wasn't going to change her to one. When he walked up onto the porch, he could smell the vampire, and this one wasn't Stephan. When she opened the door, he walked in without speaking to her.

Jimmy pulled her body to his and leaned into her ear. The sharp point of something in his ribs had him pause, but he held her to him. "There's been a strange vamp at your door. Do you know any besides Stephan?"

Her foot connected with the top of his foot almost as soon as he took her lobe into his mouth. Jimmy had only meant to tell her the information and let her go, but her flesh had been right there. When he let her go, she took several steps back before he noticed that there were several people in the room with them, two of which were her parents.

"Come on in, Jimmy. We were just discussing Gab coming to stay with us for a while." Jimmy growled low, but the older man either didn't hear him or didn't care. But Gab did.

"You hurt them and I'll tear you apart." The threat was there, and he knew that she meant every word of it. He took a step toward her when he saw that Kennedy was there too. She looked like she'd just been told the best joke, and Jimmy was going to murder her mate for it. Samuel had told Kennedy everything.

"I want you to come inside and meet some friends of Gab's. Some of them you might know, but this is John. John is her personal guard. He's going to be staying here with her at night to make sure no one—"

"No he's not," Gab declared. Jimmy flushed. "No one is going to be staying here but me. And that's final."

"You think so do you? Well, I think you're dead wrong." He looked at Gab and saw the murderous look in her eye as she pulled her gun.

"Shall I show you just how dead I can make you?"

Jimmy felt his wolf snarl at him, and before he could think about what he was doing, he stepped to Gab and pulled her to his body. When she started to protest, he took her mouth again. This time he wasn't stopping, because he had to mark her. Her hands curled into his hair, and he hesitated before moving down to her throat to nip at her, thinking that would be enough, when she curled her fingers into his hair. He thought for sure she was going to tear his head off, but all she did was hold him closer. Jimmy rocked into her soft folds and she moaned.

He had to taste her. Had to mark her so that no other male would take what was his. As soon as he licked a path from her chin to her pounding pulse, he knew that he was lost. And more than that, he was going to regret this for the rest of his life. Letting a little of his beast come to the surface, he felt his canines drop. Sinking them into her heated flesh made his cock swell more. He was in deep trouble here.

As soon as her blood filled his mouth, he swallowed. She tasted better than anything he'd ever tasted before. His wolf howled out as he drank deeply from her, giving his wolf a taste of her as well. When he sealed the ragged wound at her throat, he took her mouth again, no longer caring that he was in a room full of people and caring less that this was only the beginning to a major mistake. He wanted to fuck her right here and right now.

"Bedroom?" She looked at him, dazed, and he repeated himself. When she shook her head, he nipped at her throat again and told her to tell him.

"Jimmy?" He snarled at the person who dared touch him. Then when she slapped him, he growled. Kennedy slapped him again. "Let her go. Right now, or so help me I'll knock you on your ass."

"She's mine." His voice was harsh, not at all like himself. When she drew back again, he grabbed her arm and held it. But pain was beginning to seep into his brain, and he let her go to crumble to the floor. He looked up at Gab as realization dawned on him. She'd kicked his balls up around his throat. "It's too late for you now. Too late for the both of us."

He saw her foot coming toward him. Knew in the back of his mind that it was going to connect with his chin and he was going to go out like the lights. As it drew closer to him, he had a moment of clarity. Christ, almighty, she was his mate for all time.

Chapter 4

"What do you mean you don't know where she is? Of course you do. Call her. Bring her back here right now." Samuel shook his head at Janice sadly. "I will not have my daughter running around injured because you don't know how to control your men."

Samuel looked at the "men" in question. It was really only just the one, and he was as pissed at Jimmy as the Parkers were. And as soon as they left his house, he was going to tell him over and over again with his fist just how pissed he was.

"I assure you, Janice, that she's doing well. And she's safe. I'm sorry for this, but she swore that if I told anyone— and I do mean anyone—where she was that she'd come here and...and hurt me." What she'd told him was that she'd castrate him, and she'd said so in a very detailed threat. "She'll be back. This I promise—"

"You think I give a good fig what your promises to me are? They are nothing. Nothing, do you hear me? Not one single thing." She turned on Jimmy and walked to him. "You nearly raped her. Right there in front of us all, and then you bit her."

"He bit her?" Samuel looked at Jimmy, then at his mate. "No one said a word about her being bitten. When were you going to tell me this?"

"I told ye that he'd bonded with her." Kennedy came up out of her chair and marched toward him. "Aye, and ye take that tone with me and I'll make what she did to Jimmy look like child's play."

Samuel wanted to cup his balls to protect them, but he was actually afraid of drawing attention to the area. His wife could be a tad on the mean side when she got her Irish up. He nodded once and looked at Jimmy.

"Call her." Jimmy shook his head. "In the event you misunderstood me, that wasn't a request. Call her to you and see if she answers."

"I don't want a mate. It was a mistake. I should have taken better—"

Kennedy stomped to him and stood right in front of the large wolf. Samuel had a moment of fear...not for her but for his best friend.

"Aye, you should have taken a care. I tried to tell ye not to do it. Tried me best to bring yer'er beast back. But ye snarled at me like ye was an animal." Kennedy turned to him before she spoke to Jimmy again. "Call her now."

The compulsion was strong, very strong, and Jimmy could no more ignore it than if she'd been a wolf and his true alpha. Samuel knew the moment that Jimmy called to his mate and the exact moment she answered him.

"She said for me to go to hell. And while I was at it to take you with me." Jimmy started to laugh, then thought better of it when Kennedy glared at him. "I don't think she is going to listen to me."

"Well, can you blame her?" Wiley walked to Jimmy. "Can you make this thing work well enough to tell her that her father said for her to get her bottom here? I don't know how this whole thing works, mind you, but she'd better know that I mean business."

Jimmy nodded, then smiled at Wiley. "She said to tell you that she's a grown woman and has been for some time. She'll be home...I'm not going to tell you just what she said, but suffice it to say, she's got a very colorful vocabulary."

"And where do you think she got that from?" Janice glared at her husband and sat down with a huff. "This is the most...why is she hiding from all of us? Why won't she tell us where she's at? Or if she's well?"

"She's well. Spitting mad but well." Samuel let out a breath when Stephan appeared in the room. The man could make a grand entrance when he wanted to. "I've just left her. She said to tell you that she's fine, peachy as a matter of fact, but she'll be back when it suits her."

"That's my girl." Samuel had to cover his mouth and bit his tongue to not laugh at Wiley. The man was absolutely giddy with apparent relief. "She never says she's peachy unless she's ready to do some harm to someone. Yeah, she'll be fine now. I think we'll head on back to the hotel."

Samuel stood. "Wait. You're not staying here? I think it would be best if you did. She might need you and won't know where to find you."

He liked the couple. A great deal as a matter of fact. And his mother was having a good time with Janice. When Wiley shook his head, Samuel was surprised at how much he was upset by them leaving.

"We gotta get going back to the house by the weekend anyway. You've put up with us enough." Janice stood up as well as she continued her goodbyes. "Wiley has to work on Monday, and I've got a few jobs I have to do as well."

"You both work outside the home?" His mother flushed when she spoke. "I'm sorry. That didn't come out at all like I'd meant it to. I just meant that I'd thought you'd been retired by now."

"We did for a while. But after Rusty died we had some...there were some bills that came up. Ones that we...." Janice looked at her husband, clearly looking for help. He nodded once and took her hand.

"Rusty had some unpaid bills that we're paying off. We get by normally, but this trip, while we're glad to have seen Gab again...well, it sort of cost us both." He moved toward the door with his wife as he continued. "We'll be leaving tomorrow if you'd not mind telling Gab. She can come on by and see us before we have to get going."

They were out the door before anyone could say anything. Samuel looked at his mom, then at the rest of the room. When Stephan cleared his throat, everyone looked at him. The man looked like he'd been pole axed. Twice.

"She doesn't know that, does she? That they're working to pay off a dead man's debt?" Stephan shook his head at his question. "Do you pay her? And if you do, should she be sending some of it to her parents?"

"Gabriel doesn't get paid. I've tried to pay her several times, but she...." Stephan looked at him, then at Jimmy. "She thinks that getting paid for what she does for me, for us, will be blood money. She's doing this because of her brother."

"Perhaps it's time you told us what happened to him." Stephan nodded at Jimmy but didn't speak. "He didn't kill himself, did he?"

"No. He was murdered. I just...I've never searched her mind before, Gabriel's. I had to put her to sleep before I left because she was hurting again. When I was there, her brother's image popped up and I looked. She was there when he was killed. She actually did it."

"Does she know who his maker is?" Stephan nodded when Kennedy asked him. "And this man, I take it she's looking for him still. She's not killed him as you thought."

"She told me once that she'd taken care of him. And that her job now was to rid the world of us. I don't think she knew his name. Neither do I for that matter. But he's no longer a threat. I had no idea that she was involved in his death. It must have been hard on her to do that. And I had no idea that her parents were paying bills that he had. If I had, then I would have—"

"Would have what?" Stephan looked at Jimmy when his question hung here. "You would have what? Exploited her?

Had her do more missions? She's out there as a human, and you're not doing a fucking thing to protect her. She nearly got killed doing your work. And you're not even making sure that she's taken care of."

"That's enough." Samuel did not agree with what Jimmy had said, but there was no reason to take this out on the man without all the facts. She'd kept things from him as well, and now it was only coming to light because she'd been hurt.

"He's right. I was arrogant in my treatment of her. In actuality, I never considered her as anything but a replaceable human. Not until recently. I trained her just enough to get the job done and nothing more. If she were to be killed, then I'd simply find another human to take her place."

Jimmy was out of the chair and had Stephan lifted up off the floor in a heartbeat. He didn't struggle with the wolf but let him hold him. Jimmy's beast, his wolf, started to dance along his skin, and Samuel started to go forward to tell him to let him go when Stephan stopped him.

"I was wrong. And until he gets this out of his system, he'll hate me forever. We have to work together to help her. Gabriel is a danger to herself. And he could be her saving grace."

"And you're willing to die for that? Because from where I'm standing it looks to me like he's going to break your neck." Stephan looked at Jimmy and touched his forehead. He hit the floor just as Stephan did. Jimmy lay there unconscious while they all stood there.

"She's at her house. I took her there when I put her into a deep sleep." Stephan looked at him. "I would like to suggest that we put him there as well and hope that they can work out their differences."

Samuel nodded. "I'm game if you are. But if this doesn't work out between them, I'm blaming you for the whole thing."

"Agreed." They helped Stephan pick Jimmy up and they both disappeared. Samuel looked at the others in the room and smiled.

"Jimmy is so fucked."

~~~

Gab woke up screaming. Her heart was pounding in her chest, and she felt as if she was soaking wet. The dream again. It was only a dream. She nearly screamed again when suddenly there was a man in her room. A naked man as a matter of fact, and he was holding her ball bat.

"What the fuck is in here?" She couldn't take her eyes off him. He was a beautiful man, and when he repeated himself, she looked away.

"There's nothing in here. I had a fright." She looked at him, then away quickly. Christ, he was huge. "What are you doing here anyway?"

"I woke up here about an hour ago. I was just resting when I heard you scream." She heard the bat being set on her dresser as he continued. "As to why I'm here, I can guess and I'm going to make him pay when I find him."

"Do you think you could get something on?" He told her that they'd taken his clothes. "Well, find something to put on. You're making me nervous."

He was making her a lot of things, but nervous wasn't one of them. And when he chuckled, she thought he knew it too. Glancing his way again, she nearly cried out when she realized that he'd moved across the room and was standing very close to her.

"How nervous do I make you, Gab?" He leaned to her, and she could feel his breath on her cheek. "I can smell you now. You're aroused. Wet too I would bet."

"I don't know what you're talking about." But she squirmed on the bed. "Get out of my room please?"

He moved his finger along her bare shoulders. Her clothes had been removed as well, but when she'd gotten up during the night to use the bathroom, she'd pulled on the first thing she could find. It wasn't like her to sleep naked, and finding herself that way at three in the morning had bothered her somewhat. But now she knew. Someone had made sure that they were both naked.

"Are you hurting?" She looked up at him and was relieved to see that he'd put one of her blankets around himself. Not that it helped all that much. The man was an Adonis when it came to his chiseled chest.

"I hurt some. I'd very much like to take a shower. Why don't you call someone to come and get you so you can get out of here?"

"I've tried. All morning. I've even tried to communicate with Samuel. He's blocking me as well." Gab wasn't one hundred percent sure what he meant, but she was willing to guess it had to do with telepathy. "And you don't seem to have a phone."

"I can't afford it, and besides, don't you have a cell or something?" She flushed when she realized that he'd have nowhere to put a phone, and cleared her thoughts of him being naked as it ran through her mind. "I'd like for you to leave please."

He was quiet for a few seconds, almost a full minute, and when he did speak, she looked up at him to see if he was serious. Apparently he was, and she stared at him as he repeated his request.

"Do you have a robe I can wear? I want to make some breakfast, and as much as I don't mind being naked with you, I don't think it will solve anything. I don't want a mate." She pointed to the bathroom door and he walked to it. The blanket was only covering his front so she got a nice view of his ass. When he turned, she was caught staring at him, and no amount of lying was going to keep him from laughing at her, so she said nothing. He walked out of the room with her blue robe on that was not nearly big enough for him. She moved slowly to the shower, wondering what the fuck she was supposed to do now.

Her body ached. The bleeding had stopped and the stitches were holding, but she simply hurt. After taking her shower, she didn't have the energy to put the bandages back on, so she pulled a shirt over her head and hoped that they wouldn't seep through it. The shorts she had on were big enough for three of her, but then so was her shirt. Nothing she owned fit her and she liked it that way. Jimmy was standing at the stove when she entered.

"I've noticed that you don't have a coffee maker. Or coffee for that matter. You don't drink it?" She shook her head and reached for the pain reliever on the counter. He took the bottle from her when she couldn't get it open. "How badly do you hurt?"

"Like I wish I was hooked up to something a good deal stronger than this." She swallowed four of them dry and sat down. "When are you leaving?"

"I'm not able to." She looked up at him. "I'm ordered to stay here and protect you until you're where you can do so yourself."

"Who ordered you?" He told her Samuel did. "Well, you call him right back and tell him to fuck off. I don't need protection. I'm fine."

He didn't say anything as he sat a large plate of food in front of her. There had to have been five scrambled eggs, ten slices of bacon, and at least that much in links of sausage. He'd even fried up some potatoes, as well as sliced a tomato. She looked at his plate that was just as full.

"You don't really expect me to eat this, do you? I don't eat this much food in a week." He took a bite of his eggs and grinned at her. "You're not right."

"I am. And you need your strength." She didn't know what he had in mind that she'd need to be this strong, but the look on his face made her skin tighten. "Eat, Gab. Or I will you."

He'd said it like he meant literally. She swallowed hard as she watched him put another mouthful of eggs into his mouth and chew. Every part of her body was hot, and she was sure he knew it. When he ran his fingers up her arm, then down to her pounding pulse, she closed her eyes. He was killing her.

"You're not making this any easier on me." Gab didn't bother opening her eyes when he spoke, fearful of what he'd see there. "Do you have any idea how much I want to taste you right now? Run my tongue along yours, taste the sweetness that I tasted yesterday. Have your tongue roll against mine, taking me into you. Then I want to suckle at your nipples, see if they're large or small, if they're pink or a dusty rose. And your pussy. Christ, I can smell you right now, and I want to find out if you taste as good as you smell."

"Don't do this." His chair scraped along the floor, and she knew that he was going to touch her. Fingers danced along her throat and down into her shirt. When he touched her breast, she leaned back into his waist and gave herself up to him.

"Take off your shirt for me." She shook her head, and he laughed. "Either you do it or I do."

When she gripped the table tighter, she heard him laugh again. Then she felt his hands slide down her shirt to the hem. The sound of it tearing open had her breath catch. His hiss of approval made her moan, and when he cupped her breast in his hot hands, she reached up to hold him there.

"I want you." She nodded and felt his cock as he rocked into her back. "Right now. I don't want to do this, but I can't help myself. I need to bury myself deep inside of you."

Jimmy moved from behind her, and she whimpered. Her skin felt cold, and she reached to close her shirt. But he pulled her chair around and knelt between her legs. Looking at her, he pulled her shirt off completely and dropped it on the floor.

"I'm going to taste your skin." She nodded and watched his head lower to her nipple, where he licked it. "Dusty rose and thick. Just like I'd hoped."

He suckled at her until she thought she'd scream. First one breast, then the other, licking a path between the two. Gab felt his hands grip her hips, and he pulled her forward. Then he slid his hands up her short legs and cupped her ass.

"Mine." She moaned when he spoke. "All mine. As much as I think I want you, it's not enough. I need to have you. Now. Right now, Gab."

"Please. I hurt with need." He stood up suddenly, taking her with him. Her legs wrapped around his waist like they had a mind of their own. When she felt the counter beneath her, she reached for the robe tie and tore it open. His cock was straining from his body, and a thick creamy stream dripped from the tip.

Her shorts were suddenly gone, and she sat there naked. When he took a step back, she thought he meant to leave her like this, but he pulled a chair from the table and sat it in front of her. Gab had an idea what he thought he was going to do and started to protest. But he silenced her with a kiss.

"I'm going to eat you until you fill me. Then I'm going to slam my cock deep inside of you and fuck you until neither of us can walk." His fingers moved to slide inside of her, and she cried out. "Christ, you're so tight. And wet. I'm torn now whether I want to drink from you or fuck you."

"Please." She wanted it all. She wanted him. Gab reached down and wrapped her fingers around his thickness and pulled him to her. She wanted him now. As soon as he was at her entrance, she rocked forward and took him to his crown. He slammed the rest of the way forward, taking her breath away.

"Come, baby. Come for me." Gab felt her body ready. As his teeth slid along her throat to her shoulder, he pounded into her. When he told her to come with him, he sank his teeth deep into her shoulder, and she came. Christ, did she come.

Over and over she cried out his name as he took her. When he threw back his head and howled, she felt pinpoints of stars sprinkle around her vision until she knew that she was going to faint. When he bit her again, she screamed out his name and let the darkness slide over her. She was never going to be the same again, she knew it.

Chapter 5

Jimmy watched her sleep. He'd hurt her, he knew, but there was no way he was going to regret taking her. Christ, she was everything he'd never realized he wanted in a woman and then some. Smiling, he got up to clean up the kitchen. They'd left it in a shambles.

As soon as he entered the kitchen he knew that something was off. Looking around, he tried to remember things the way he'd left them, but he didn't know the room like he did his own kitchen. But something was not right. Jimmy saw him seconds before he became solid.

"What the fuck are you doing here?" Jimmy tried to get his heart to calm down and his wolf as well when Stephan sat down. "She's sleeping."

"I would guess she needs it." There was a tone there, full of humor, but Jimmy decided to ignore it. "She's going to do you a world of good, James. And you her. You'll keep each other safe."

"She's doing all right on her own." Jimmy started picking up the plates to dump when they suddenly disappeared. The kitchen was pristine as well. He sat down in the chair and glared at the coffee sitting before him. "She doesn't drink coffee. I should cut back on it too."

The coffee disappeared, and a cup of something else was sitting in its place. "She drinks tea. Not as much as she wants, but that's her favorite kind. I keep some at the office for her when she comes by. You're her mate."

KATHI S. BARTON

Jimmy didn't comment because he wasn't sure he needed to. Picking up the cup, he tasted wild berries and sweetness. He took another sip before sitting it down. Stephan put a file in front of him.

"She works for me, as you know. And I've asked Samuel and Kennedy before approaching you with this, but I'd like for you to join her. But this time I must insist that I pay you both." Jimmy nodded and opened the file. "This is all I've ever given her. She finds the nests and takes care of them. You'll need these too."

He was handed a small stack of coins, and even from where he sat, Jimmy could tell they were silver. Jimmy looked at Stephan. The man was grinning.

"As of now you are no longer affected by it. The silver kills vampires, and she has had a great deal of luck with it. I believe she puts it onto their eyes and it sort of melts into their brain. I clean the coins back up and give them back to her when I go to identify the bodies."

"What will she say about me working with her?" Jimmy didn't know why, but he didn't want to piss her off by taking the job offer without talking to her first. He looked up when Stephan didn't answer him right away. "She's going to be pissed, isn't she?"

"Yes." Jimmy touched the stack of coins and didn't feel the burn that he normally would. It would be nice to be able to not be fearful of silver. All his life he'd been afraid of having it cut into his flesh, and had avoided it as much as he could. He shook his head at Stephan.

"I'll talk to her. If she approves, I'll think about it. I'm not going to...." He got up to pace. The kitchen, like the rest of the house, was entirely too small for a man his size, but she was here. "I didn't want a mate, and now that I have one I'm not sure what the fuck I'm supposed to do. Protect her yeah, but what else? She's braver than I am. Smarter too if you want to know the truth. This place? I think she owns it and the property around it. And her own business. I have an

56

apartment that I'm seldom in and can't remember the last time I ran a vacuum cleaner in it."

"So you think that because you're a slob and not as book smart as her that it makes you less her mate?" Stephan laughed before Jimmy could agree with him. "You're just what she needs, and she is the same for you. Destiny put the two of you together for a reason. Sometimes the reasons aren't clear, but there are reasons."

"She's going to hate me in a few months. I'm a pain in the ass." Stephan nodded. "You know you could disagree with me once or twice when I'm insulting myself."

"Would you? I doubt it. You're a stubborn man and a more stubborn wolf." Stephan stood up. "Talk to her and get back to me. She knows now how to contact me."

Stephan started toward the door and turned back. He seemed to be listening to something, and Jimmy listened as well. He could hear her heart beating in the other room, slow and steady. Stephan frowned.

"I've convinced her parents to stay for a few more days. I've also made sure that they no longer have to worry about money. But...." He looked out the door, then back at Jimmy before he continued. "Something isn't right about this thing with her brother. I'm not sure of what the bills were that they told us about, but I cannot find a single thing that the young man had owed money on. I'd like to talk to you both about this as well."

Jimmy nodded and closed the door behind the man when he stepped out. He was turning out the lights when he felt someone touch his mind. He stiffened when he realized it was Samuel.

"Stephan said to tell you that the pantries are stocked and the freezer is as well." He waited for him to continue. *"I'm sorry. I shouldn't have done to you what we did. I'm glad it worked out for you, but it was wrong."*

"We're fine. Or at least I hope we are." He opened the refrigerator and saw that not only was it stocked, but it was

nearly bursting with food. The smallish freezer was as well. *"We're staying for a while, are we?"*

"You need to get her healed up. I've had word that there is something coming your way. It seems that a few vampires are gathering a group up to come after her." Jimmy wondered why it hadn't happened before now. *"She's going to need to be strong, both of you are."*

After a few more minutes of setting up a time to get together, Jimmy asked him about working for Stephan. He still planned on talking with Gab about it, but he wanted his friend's opinion.

"You couldn't do any better than to work for him. And he will pay you well. I guess he has the backing of some council behind this." Jimmy made his way to the bedroom as Samuel continued. *"Also it will help you keep an eye on your mate. She's a little headstrong I guess."*

"You think?" Jimmy laughed with Samuel as he looked down at her. *"She's beautiful. I don't know why I fought so hard against this. It's not so bad."*

"No, it's not. And it only gets better as time goes on." Samuel chuckled as he continued. *"Of course she might still try to rip your throat out, but for now, she's content."*

Jimmy crawled into bed with her. It was too small, but he was content to snuggle up to her to make room. He heard Samuel laugh but ignored him. The only thing the man could think about was he had no sense of holding a fine woman. Closing his eyes, he wondered again why he'd fought so hard at this. Sleep claimed him quickly.

~~~

Samuel was called to the door by Butler. The man was beside himself with worry and he'd dropped everything to see what was going on. As soon as he was near the door, he hesitated. There were several vampires on the other side of the door.

"They can't enter unless you invite them. Don't." He wanted to tell Stephan no shit but was kind of glad he'd

reminded him of the fact. Samuel opened the door and stared at the first man. There were six more behind him.

"I'd like a word with you, Lord Payne." Samuel crossed his arms over his chest and waited. He never batted an eye when the man gestured to the inside of his house. "Will you invite us in? It is customary to do so."

"No." Samuel watched the other men as they spread out around the first man. "You try something and you'll be dead before the sun comes up."

"You're going to threaten us? You've no idea why we're here. Perhaps it is a social call and nothing more." The man smiled and showed his fangs. Samuel wasn't impressed. "Shall I show you that I mean you no harm?"

"You can show me all you want, but it means shit to me. Say what you think I want to hear and get the hell off my property." The man stiffened but nodded. "Be quick about it. I've things to do, and hanging around a bunch of blood suckers isn't on the list of shit I need to get taken care of."

"You're very hostile, are you not? But it matters little. We wish to speak with the one that is known as the Silver Queen." He smiled again, this time minus the fangs. "We have a warrant for her arrest."

"I don't know who you'd be talking about." He had an idea it was Gab but was not sure. He'd heard she used silver to hunt with but nothing more. And he was sure he'd never heard anyone refer to her as the Silver Queen.

"If you harbor a known criminal element, it will go badly for you." Samuel took a step forward when the man threatened him. All of them, including the man talking, took two back. "You're not scaring us."

"Really?" Samuel let a little of his cat go, just enough that his own fangs dropped and his hands morphed into sharp talons. "I think you're scared shitless. And you should be, too, because right now there are twenty or so of my men right behind you."

The man turned slowly and looked at the yard. Samuel had no idea who most of the wolves and cats were that were in his yard, but he knew that if he needed them to, they'd leap at these men. Jimmy whispered in his mind just as he was about to speak.

"They belong to you now. As of this morning as a matter of fact. I meant to tell you." Samuel started to tell him thanks when Jimmy continued. *"You'll meet the ones you don't know today after lunch. They're ready to pledge to you."*

"You do know that I'm a lion, right? Are they aware of that too?" He told him they were. *"And what the fuck am I supposed to do with a pack of wolves?"*

"I think what they're doing now." Samuel decided he was going to kill the pup when he saw him next. But right now he had a bunch of vamps to contend with. Pulling his cat back, he took another step to the door just as Kennedy came around the corner of their house as a cat. The vampires disappeared.

"Were you trying to get yourself killed?" he snapped at her when they were alone. "I'd never been so terrified in my life when I saw you there."

"I was out on a run, as I've told ye thirty times now. I only came around the corner then because no one was in the kitchen *a ligean* meself in. Would you have rather I'd been naked when I saw them?" He tried to rein in his temper when she poked him in the chest. "Butler was standing behind the door with a shotgun filled with *grán grán trom*, Brigitte was standing behind him with a handful of our silver, and you were talking to the fucking bastards like ye were inviting them to *tae*."

Her Irish was bleeding through quite a bit now, and he knew better than to point it out to her. Whenever she was pissed like she was right now, he had a hard time understanding her. He was getting better, but not every word made sense right now. Like he knew that *tae* was tea and that *ligean* was let.

"*Grán grán trom?*" She told him buckshot. "Ah. Well that's good. I thought maybe your *seanmháthair* was here again."

Kennedy hit him. "You drive me nuts." He noticed that she'd said each word carefully, as if she was afraid of saying something he might not understand. Samuel hated when she did that. He loved her Irish temper and language. "What will we *dhéanamh* now? We canna turn her over to them."

"And we won't. And until she's healthy, we'll make sure they can't find her on their own either." He pulled her into his lap and held her. "I was so terrified when I saw you there."

"I scared them as well." He laughed with her. "I dinna know they could come out this late in the day. I thought them to be having issues with the sun."

"It's because they're old." Stephan bowed before them. "My Lady. I'm sorry I didn't warn you about them. But to be honest I had no idea that they knew she'd ever been here. I'm thinking that her parents were the ones that told them. They've no idea what's going on."

"We need to bring them here." Stephan nodded his agreement. "And Jimmy and Gab, will they be safe where they are?"

"They are. For now. I've made sure that her scent is not anything they can follow. As soon as I have yours and James's permission, I'll do the same for him. It will not keep them completely safe from them, but it will slow them down." Stephan sat down, and Samuel noticed that he looked exhausted.

"You're not supposed to be awake, are you?" Stephan shook his head. "When was the last time you fed? I would bet it's been a while."

"It has. I have been preoccupied of late. I will take care of it today." Samuel put out his wrist. "I cannot take from you like this, my friend. I will…I'm nearly starved."

"You'll do it or I'll make you." Samuel didn't know if he could really make the vamp do it or not, but he waited. When he reached for him, Samuel held his breath as he licked the vein. The bite was almost nothing compared to what he thought it would be.

He drank for a few minutes before sealing the wound. When he leaned back in the chair, Samuel could see that his color was back and that he looked much better. He started to ask him if he'd had enough when Stephan spoke.

"Your blood is rich, my friend. Like champagne from some of the finest wineries. You've helped me a great deal." Embarrassed, Samuel nodded. "I will have a connection to you now. Stronger than before. You are aware of that, are you not?"

"I am." Samuel was startled when Stephan held out his own wrist after cutting it open with his nail. "You don't need to do that."

"But I do. And I'd wish to offer it to your mate and mother as well. We need to know we can contact each other even when there is no way for us to speak." Samuel looked at Kennedy. She nodded and took the offered wrist. Samuel took a few sips as well when Stephan did the same for him.

The connection was immediate and profound. There was a link between them now stronger than he thought he had with his own mate. When he looked at Stephan, he seemed just as shocked.

"It would seem that you and I are going to have a better link than I thought. Your mate doesn't have the same, but I would bet that she will be able to contact me no matter where she is. Even as deep underground as she can go." Samuel wasn't sure that was a good thing or not and told him so. *"I shall never intrude on your thoughts with your mate, my dear friend. We will only be able to communicate if*

the need arises or you wish to shoot the shit, as I've heard it called."

"Just so long as you know that I will shoot you if you get her hurt." Stephan nodded and stood up. "I shall go now. I have a great deal to do today, and once the young Gabriel rises, it will double. She will not be happy with her enforced confinement. Or maybe she will. I believe the two of them, James and her, have worked things out to their satisfaction."

After he left, Samuel sat in the kitchen for a while. Kennedy had a phone call she had to take, so he sat there thinking about his life. He'd only moved here to get away from the place his father had lived. Now he had a pack, a pride, and who knew what else in the way of species. Today showed him that he was going to have to take control of this or he was going to be overrun with people he had no idea what to do with. He looked up when his mom came into the room.

"Did you know that there is a pack of wolves running around the property?" He nodded at her. "I wondered. There are at least thirty of them roaming right outside the house. Are we being invaded?"

She'd been joking but he nodded anyway. "There are people that are looking for Gab, Jimmy's mate. They want her for crimes against them, I guess."

"I see. And will we be taking a stand with her with the wolves then?" Samuel nodded. "Good. I like a good fight as much as the next person, but having help will only make us stronger."

"There might be a few more too. Other than wolves. Last night I was approached by a panther and his family. They want to stay here as well. I'm thinking it's a good thing we bought the Savage campground."

Last year he'd been given the rights to purchase the three hundred acres that the campground sat on. He'd thought about turning it down, but Kennedy had talked him into buying it and having the Savages run it for them.

Kennedy said it would be a good investment. Right now it was becoming a haven for those that wanted to join him. Samuel wondered if there was another pack/pride like his. He doubted it very much.

"I'm going into town later." He looked at his mom when she spoke. "I've a few things to take care of that can't wait, and I would like to see about getting some things for the new couple. Do you think they'll live in her house? It's very tiny."

Samuel had never been there but had heard that it was small. He wondered about the property too. There was some land that surrounded the house, but he didn't know who owned it. He made a mental note to check on it.

"I'm going in later as well. Do you want to hitch a ride with me? I can tie your chair to the back of my car if you want." She grinned at him. "And if you can talk Kennedy into going too, I'll take my favorite women out to dinner."

"I'll see what I can do." She started to roll away when she stopped and looked at him. "I've been thinking about the men who were here earlier. The vampires. Do you suppose they might get Gab's parents?"

"I've sent men to get them now. I think they would be safer here. If there are any issues with them coming, do you think you could help?" She nodded. "Thanks, Mom."

"I love you, son. And it's my pleasure to help you." After she left him alone, he moved back to his office. He had to make a few phone calls as well as set up a meeting with Gab and Jimmy. She needed to pledge to him, and Jimmy needed to decide on where he was going to work. Either way he chose, Samuel was going to be happy. They were a family right now. All of them.

Samuel was just closing down his computer two hours later when his mother came back. She was smiling, and before he could ask, Kennedy came into the room. Both of them had dressed up, and he felt shabby in his jeans and tee-shirt. Grinning, he asked them if he had time to change.

"Yes, but wear a tie please. I think we're going to a *ceiliúradh*, a celebration. I've spoken with Jimmy and he's going to ask Gab to marry him tonight. Her parents are going to come to dinner with us." Kennedy kissed him as she continued. "We're going to help them with their *baile* too if you don't mind. The one they have is a might smallish for a new family, don't you think?"

He kissed her nose and nodded. Things were looking better all the time. He just hoped that it continued. But he'd been in business long enough to know that things didn't always go along nicely like you wanted them to. Life was not very much different. Taking the stairs three at a time, he made his way to his bedroom. He'd be wearing a tie for the first time since his own wedding.

Chapter 6

Gab wasn't used to sharing her space with anyone, especially a large man like Jimmy. And he was constantly touching her. She wouldn't mind that so much if it didn't heat her up to the point of nearly throwing him to the bed again and having her way with him. The man was just too sexy for his own good.

"You're upset again." She glared at him when he spoke. "I'm sorry, but maybe we should think of adding onto your house. I'm not...it's smaller than my apartment."

"It's because it's not supposed to be shared by two people no matter what the realtor said." She took a deep breath. "I've lived alone for a long time. I'm just not used to this. You're so here."

He laughed, and she did as well. They were going to dinner with his boss, and she was nervous about what they'd think of her as his mate. Gab knew that they were now—mates—but what would they think of him taking a human as one? She dropped her brush and bent to pick it up when he moved behind her.

"I would love to take you like this." His voice moved over her like a caress. "If you hold onto the counter, I can make short work of these pants."

"We don't have time for this." He rocked into her again, and she moaned. "Jimmy, I can't do this right now. I'm still...I hurt still."

He backed from her almost too quickly, and she staggered slightly. When he pulled her back to his body, she watched him in the mirror as he pulled her shirt down. She'd covered the wounds up with tape and gauze, but they were bleeding again. He pulled the tape back and kissed her shoulder.

"I can heal these for you. Not completely but almost." She watched him as he licked her wound. "My saliva will heal them much faster than you can."

"You'll get sick," she told him as he leaned down and nipped at her shoulder before licking along the wound again. Gab felt the soreness dissipate and then watched as the tear in her skin seemed to close on its own. When he lifted her shirt up and did the same to the one on her side, she moaned. Christ, this was almost as good as sex.

"Take off your pants." She nodded and tried to work the snap. Finally, he tore them open, and the sound of the button pinging off the mirror had her breathing hard. "I'm going to enjoy this. As soon as I'm finished I'm going to eat you. I've missed being able to do that last night."

Nodding because she was unable to speak, she held onto the counter while he took care of the wound on her leg. She was burning up with need, and when he turned her around, she took his mouth with hers.

"Sit on the counter. I need you." She moaned and moved to sit on the sink. The bathroom was the perfect size for this kind of play, as he was able to touch her while he sat on the commode. As soon as her panties were off, he buried his head between her legs and suckled her clit.

Her climax startled a scream from her. When she came again a few seconds later, she nearly begged him to stop. She couldn't catch her breath, much less control her heart rate. Jimmy brought her to peak three more times before he spread her thighs wide open and looked at her that way.

"Christ, you're lovely. I could feast like this forever." She tried to close her legs, embarrassed, but he held her open. "No, don't. I want to watch you come this way. See your pretty pussy when you come again."

His fingers danced along her thighs to her clit and then slid inside of her. Gab was trying her best not to scream again, but he pinched her clit and she came, screaming out his name. When his tongue entered her, lapping at her sweet spot, she had to hold onto the counter or fall off. Her body was a mass of tremors.

"I'm going to fuck you now." He stood up and opened his pants, and his cock sprang free. But she wanted to taste him as he did her and reached for him. Jimmy stopped her by closing his hand over hers. "You do and I'm going to come all over you. And as much as that appeals to me right now, I've very much like to take you from behind."

He helped her stand and leaned her over the counter. Watching him in the mirror, he grinned at her. She nearly came from his smile.

"I wish you were my bitch." She moaned when he slid his cock near her pussy. "I'm going to enjoy taking you to the woods out back and us fucking as wolves. Running you down and biting you while I come deep inside of you."

He moved into her slowly. She moaned as he moved in and out of her, going deeper with each stroke. When he pressed her head down to the counter, she felt him lean over her, and his breath scorched her back. His finger sliding over her clit had her cry out, and when he moved inside of her with his cock he bit her.

"*Mine*," he whispered in her mind. "Tell me, Gab. Tell me you belong to me. Forever. Tell me."

"I'm yours. Christ, I'm all yours." He pulled from her, turned her around, and entered her. Picking her up by her ass, he took her hard against the wall.

"Bite me. When you come, I want you to bite me and draw blood. Drink from me until we both come together." She nodded and he stiffened suddenly. "I'm coming, love. Bite."

She didn't even think about the fact that she'd hurt him. The thought of sinking her teeth into his flesh made her hungry for him. When she tasted his blood, hot and spiked with his wolf, she screamed out his name around his wound and came. His teeth biting into her made her see stars again, and as she slid from this world into darkness again, she thought that she heard him say he loved her.

Jimmy was just putting her on the bed when she woke. There was a coppery taste in her mouth, and she licked her lips. She could taste him there still and looked at him when he laughed.

"I belong to you now, you know that, right?" She'd thought that's what she'd done but it was good to know for sure. "I want you again. I know you're more than likely sore, but you've no idea how much I'd like to say fuck this dinner thing and stay right here with you."

"Can we?" He shook his head. "I guess not. Especially since my mom and dad are going to be there." She started to stand, but a wave of dizziness washed over her. Jimmy grabbed her before she fell.

"Are you all right?" She started to nod but was afraid it would make her sick. "I think you should just sit here for a minute."

She didn't have to agree because her knees buckled and she fell back. Jimmy was saying her name over and over, but she was too busy trying to not throw up on him when she felt the world tumble around her. Before she knew it, she was out. *Christ, that was some sex*, she thought as her body went limp.

~~~

"I told you, I don't fucking know what happened. I was helping her up when she suddenly pitched forward. If I hadn't been there, she would have fallen on her face." Samuel tried not to laugh at Jimmy as he explained what had happened. At least he explained most of it. The room smelled of sex, and his shirt was buttoned up wrong. Plus, he was pretty sure that Gab was naked under the blanket.

"You've called the clinic to ask them to send someone." Jimmy growled at him, and Samuel had to bite his lip hard. This was more fun than it should have been. "Look, I'm trying to help you."

"I know, but what the fuck, Samuel. She's out. I mean really out. I can't even get her to open her eyes." Jimmy started pacing and must have noticed that his shirt was buttoned wrong. He looked at Samuel as he redid them. "We had sex, in the event you've not figured it out. She bit me. I don't know enough about having a mate to know if she's being converted or I've hurt her somehow. She's scaring the shit out of me."

"She'll be fine. Her pulse is good and strong, and she's...you sealed her wounds?" He nodded and Samuel looked at the girl. "Jimmy, how much of your blood has she had?"

"I don't know. A bit, I guess. Why?" Samuel didn't know a great deal about converting a human to wolf either, but it only took three exchanges to make it happen for a lion. And if they'd had sex and exchanged blood, he'd say that he'd converted her without knowing it.

The doctor showed up about then, and lucky for them both he was a wolf. In seconds he told them that she was resting and that as soon as she woke, her wolf would be starving. Jimmy sat down hard in the chair and put his head between his legs.

"I didn't ask her. She's going to be pissed when she wakes up." Samuel didn't know what to say so he said nothing to Jimmy and showed the doctor out. When he came back, Jimmy was still sitting in the chair and Gab was awake, just pulling a large shirt over her head. She didn't say anything when he asked her if she was all right. She didn't get a chance to answer because Jimmy moved to her.

"Baby, I'm so sorry." Jimmy took her hands into his. "I didn't mean to do this, you have to know that." Gab looked at him over Jimmy's shoulder with a questioning look.

"He converted you. You're now a wolf." She stood up so suddenly that Jimmy hit the floor. Samuel backed up. There was no way he was going to be in the line of fire if there was going to be one. When she sat down again, he watched her closely. He didn't want to have to hurt her, but if she went nuts about this, he was going to have to do something.

"How does one convert another person without their consent?" Samuel looked at Jimmy, who was just standing up. "Don't touch me just yet. I'm having a major overload right now and I'm not sure that you touching me is going to help."

"It will." Samuel nodded to Jimmy to tell him to go ahead while he spoke softly to Gab. "You need his touch because you're his mate. His wolf will need you too."

"I don't think I want him to—" Jimmy put his hands on her bare arms and she moaned. Gab turned in his arms and buried her nose in his neck. Kennedy had done the same to him when she'd been converted. *This part must be universal*, he thought.

He started to walk out of the bedroom to give them some privacy when he saw that Kennedy was standing there. She walked to him and put her arms around him and he held her.

"When he started screaming in my mind that he'd killed her, I nearly had a heart attack." Kennedy nodded as he continued. "Then when he said that she'd fainted and that he couldn't wake her, I thought the vamps had gotten to her somehow. I'd never been so scared in my life but in those few seconds."

"You just left me. I was afraid too," Kennedy said. Samuel pulled her tighter to his body as she cried softly to him. "I tried to contact Gab, but I hit a wall, and when I reached out to Jimmy, I couldn't…his mind was a mess."

"He was afraid for her." Kennedy nodded. "I was too. But he'd changed her. She's a wolf. How she takes it is anyone's guess, but for now they seem to be fine." He heard them before he saw them, and when he turned he could see the difference in Gab right away. She practically glowed.

"She's really hungry." Samuel nodded, and Kennedy went to her when Jimmy spoke again. "I think we'll still go out with you if it's not too late."

"It's not. We have time." Kennedy hugged Gab and smiled at her as she continued. "I bought you something. It's not much, but I wanted you to have it. I hope it fits."

"Fits? You didn't buy me a dress, did you?" Kennedy nodded at Gab, and she groaned. "I don't do dresses. I barely do clothes that fit. I can't wear it."

"You will because your parents are going to be there. And I'll help you. I didn't buy you high heels, but I got you something flat. You'll have to work up to heels."

"High heels? Lady, do you have any idea the kind of damage those suckers do to your legs? Not to mention all the damage I'm going to do when I have to fall on my face." The door to the bedroom closed behind the women. Samuel looked at Jimmy.

"You okay?" Jimmy nodded, then shook his head. "Just so you know, it doesn't get any easier about the worrying part. No matter what they do, we're going to worry about our mates."

"You do know that that isn't helping me right now, right?" Jimmy scrubbed his hand over his face. "I've never been so afraid in my entire life. I never wanted a mate. Never in my wildest dreams did I think I'd ever take one, but Christ…."

"Yeah." Samuel sat down in the chair and looked around the room. "Jimmy, this is the littlest house I think I've ever been in. Did it once belong to a kid for their toys?"

They both laughed. Jimmy looked around too as if he'd never been in this room before. "It sort of suits her. I mean, not in the size, but the stuff in here. Or what little there is in here. You should see the kitchen. There's the usual stuff like refrigerator and stove, but it has a table that is attached to the wall that closes up when not in use. Otherwise, you'd not be able to wash the dishes. I'm going to see if she wants to build deeper in the woods. Something much bigger."

If a person just looked at him, they'd never know, but Jimmy was very wealthy. He'd made it big a few years ago in an investment that no one but him had believed in. Apparently he'd ended up buying the company, and all he did now was hang around and work odd jobs when it suited him. Like working for Samuel as an enforcer.

"I'm in love with her." Samuel looked at Jimmy when he spoke. "I mean, I guess it's sort of soon to be thinking that, but she's everything to me. Prickly, stubborn, and a tad on the violent side, but she makes me want to be a better man."

"I can understand that. Kennedy does the same for me. She has all this money that should make her something of a snob, but she's just as down to earth as any person. I love her with all my heart. And I can't think of what it would be like without her. And with the baby on the way?" Samuel smiled. "It's like I'm living in a wonder world."

"You're a sap." Jimmy laughed at him. "Christ, who would have thought it. Now all we have to do is get Kaleb a mate. Or laid. Maybe if he got laid once in a while he'd be a little less intense."

Samuel didn't think that Kaleb would ever loosen up, and he'd most certainly never find himself a mate. Not the way he was. The man could hardly stand to be in the same room with an unattached female, much less have one in his bed. He was serious about never getting a mate, and Samuel had a feeling that he'd murder the female that dared to smell like one to him.

"I'm thinking that with all this that's going on, you should not take that job." Samuel had been thinking about the new members to his pride and the fact that they'd be hunting vampires. Not that he had anything against them— he actually had quite a few vampires as friends—but rogues were dangerous and strong. And most of the time they didn't give a shit about who or how they killed to get what they wanted.

"We've not even talked about it. I don't think I want her to do it anymore, but then I'm thinking that saying that to Gab would be the equivalent of telling her to do it. As I've said, she's sort of stubborn." Jimmy started pacing as he continued. "But I've also been thinking that they know her now, wouldn't you think?"

"They do." Jimmy looked at him, and Samuel hastened to tell him. "They came to the house the other day looking for the Silver Queen. I thought of her immediately since she uses silver coins to kill them. They didn't know her name, and I didn't invite them in or anything, but it was a little scary when Kennedy came back from a run just as they were threatening me. I thought for sure I was going to get into a rumble with them."

Samuel had tried for a joke, but it failed miserably. Jimmy sat down and stared at him for several seconds before he spoke. Samuel had a feeling he'd been working up to this for a while now.

"I've spoken to Stephan. He's given me the ability to touch and handle silver. He also plans to take away my scent. I'm not sure how he does it, but I can smell Gab now when I'm not sure you can." Samuel shook his head, telling him he'd not had her scent since he'd met her.

"I think you should also know that Stephan took my blood today. He came by the house and was exhausted. I think...he said he'd like to take some of all of us so that he could find us when needed. He even took a few sips of my mom's." Jimmy nodded but said nothing as he continued. "I think he's already taken some of Gab's too."

"I'll talk to him about mine soon. I don't want to have to get into a position where no one can find us. With him having our blood, at least he'd be able to locate us even if we're dead."

The car pulling into the drive had them both stand. Samuel knew that Gab's parents were going to meet them there with his mom, but he was still on alert since the whole thing with the vamps. When the Parkers got out of the car and moved up onto the porch, Samuel had to laugh. They were the oddest couple of human's he'd ever met. And apparently his mom thought so as well, as she was trying her best not to laugh as the two of them fussed at each other.

"I told you not to wear that tie. Do you even listen to a darned thing I tell you?" Wiley nodded at his wife as if she'd been doing this for years. "And that suit looks like you've had it nearly since we were married."

"I have. And it is the one we were married in. I think I look just fine. What's wrong with this tie? You gave it to me." The tie in question looked to be from the early seventies and was as brightly colored as a box of crayons. All the colors too. "And there are some of the colors of the shirt in it."

The shirt did have some of the colors of the tie in it. Samuel was pretty sure that it also had some lunch on it as well. While the tie was a large paisley pattern, the shirt was plaid. And the suit looked like he'd bought it from the rack about two sizes too small.

"What do you think people will say when they find out that you've been wearing those same shoes since you bought them forty years ago?" Samuel put his hand over his mouth to cover the laugh when Wiley looked at his shoes his wife pointed out. "You should have polished them."

"Then, my dear wife, everyone would have been looking at my old shiny shoes instead of the loveliest woman in the room." Wiley kissed her quickly on the mouth and moved up to the porch. Janice was still standing there when Wiley took his hand. "Shut her up, didn't I?"

"You did at that. And the next time my wife fusses at me about my attire, I'm going to use that line." Wiley laughed with him and stopped in mid laugh. Samuel looked over his shoulder at Jimmy, then in the direction he was looking. "Mother of God."

To say that his wife had worked a miracle would have been an understatement. He wouldn't even have recognized Gab had he not carried the dress she had on out to the car when they left and knew what it looked like. The dark maroon color of the dress suited the woman like the color had been designed specifically for her. And the way it fit her body left no doubt that she was a woman.

"You look...." He glanced at Jimmy as he started to tell her what a vision she made and was tempted to close the man's mouth. But Jimmy moved toward Gab as if he was a man on a mission.

"Kennedy insisted on putting make-up on me." Gab looked around shyly as she continued. "I feel like a fool. If you want me to take it off I can—"

Jimmy pulled Gab into his arms and cut her off with a kiss. He was still devouring her when Stephan showed up. Samuel thought he was going to have to hose them down when they made their way to the awaiting cars. This was going to be fun, Samuel just knew it.

Chapter 7

"We have to kill her before she gets her strength back. If we don't, she's gonna keep on killing us faster than we can make more of us." Valda LaRue looked at the idiot in front of her. He'd been prattling on for the past hour about this Silver Queen and they were no closer to getting an answer about what to do about her than before. And as much as they bitched about the woman, Valda had more reasons for wanting her dead. She'd killed her mate.

Valda wasn't as old as some of the vampires that were in this room with her. In fact, she'd be considered a baby compared to some of them at only one hundred and ten years old. But she had balls and she was strong. The rest of them, all of them really, bowed down to her. And she loved it.

"And where do you propose we find her? Do you have a crystal ball in your hand that will point the way to her?" She wanted to kick out at the man there, but didn't. "I don't see any of you making any headway into locating the girl, much less killing her. We cannot do one without the other. And finding her has been our biggest stumbling block."

"The lion said that he'd kill us if we returned." Valda glanced at the man who had spoken. She thought his name was Peter but wasn't sure, so nodded at him to continue. "We went as a force as you suggested, but he didn't seem bothered by it. There were wolves there as well. At least two dozen."

Valda hated wolves. Not only were they nasty dogs, but they didn't care if they tore at your face or your body so long as they killed. She shivered when she thought about one of them biting her.

"When will you return?" The man looked around the room as if he was looking for someone to back him up. "Surely you're not going to let a lion, a simple cat, dictate to you where to find this woman, are you?"

"My lady, he has wolves at his beck and call. What if he should call them to him when we return?" She snorted. "He did seem to have a great deal of control over them."

"No one has control over wolves, especially not a lion. They are two different breeds, and there is no way that they'd bow before a cat." A memory of something she'd heard recently tickled at her mind, but it was gone before it fully formed. "Get back there tomorrow night. I want that girl killed and I've no wish to have to go and do it myself. If I do, then I would surely hate to be in your shoes."

He bowed before her, and she looked around the room as they started to plan. There were times, like now, that she wished that she'd stayed on her own. Having a nest was about like having a bunch of wasps surrounding you. All buzzing about but nothing ever getting done. She was glad now that she'd made the rule about each of them creating a child a month until they outnumbered the humans in the area. Once that was done, she had a bigger plan. Train them to rule. She wanted to have an empire of vampires working for her and supplying her with as much funding as they could while humans did all the work.

Valda wasn't a human hater. No, never that. They were much too valuable to them as a food source as well as helpmates during the hours when they needed to rest. Hers had made that point very clear recently when she'd woken early to find her bringing all matter of men into her home and using her house as a brothel. They needed to be able to punish the infidels, not simply fire them. Of course, she'd made an example of the bitch even though it was against the rules of her kind, but that had been too much fun to think of as breaking a rule.

"My lady?" She looked at her manservant. "There is a call for you. I do believe it is the council. They wish a word with you about a gathering."

Nodding, she followed him out. If the man walked any straighter he'd look like a poker. She giggled slightly when she thought of him standing next to her fireplace ready to stoke up the fire. He left her to her phone in the office a few seconds later. Whoever was calling her at two in the morning had to be carrying bad news. She dreaded the call with all that she was.

"Lady La Rue. Rumor has it that you've assembled tonight." She rolled her eyes. "You know that in order to do so you must obtain a permit. And give us thirty days' notice."

"I was aware of that, but as you are also aware, I've out of state friends here and they didn't let us know they were coming until they arrived." While mostly true, it was still a lie. They were friends from out of town, but she'd known for months they were coming. She looked down at her nails as she continued. "How would I ask for something like a permit when I'd had no idea they were coming?"

Because, she thought, *if I had told you they were coming, you would have required their names*. And some of the people assembled there had not wanted to give even her their name, much less allow her to put it to paper.

"This is most inconvenient on your part, I think." She wanted to tell him to fuck off, but she'd learned long ago that keeping the brass (as she'd heard them called) happy was mostly what kept her off the list of killed vamps. She'd tried her best to instill that in her mate, but he'd had a mind of his own. It was why he'd been at the house where the nest was instead of with her like she'd asked him to be.

"I've heard that you've also petitioned to have yourself instated as the new Master of the Realm in your mate's stead?" She told him she had filed last week. "Unfortunately for you, we've picked someone else to take over the realm. He will be a good deal firmer than you'd be. And while I believe you to be an effective leader, we believe you will lack the ability to carry through when it comes to punishment. Something that your late mate was very...let us just call it harsh at."

She growled low before she could stop it. His responding growl had her thinking that he'd been prepared for her getting pissed, and his next words confirmed it. Valda was going to kill this man as soon as she could gather a crew together to do so.

"Starting as soon as tonight you'll be stripped of your title as lady and you'll be removed from the house. The new master is going to be moving in straightaway and you'll just be in his way." She heard the steel in his voice. Her fangs dropped in response to it. "If I hear of you assembling again without the proper paperwork, or even gathering together for a celebration, I will send in a squad and have you and the rest of your nest killed immediately. From now on you'll follow every rule right to the letter or I will take great enjoyment in having you hunted."

"You can't do this to me. I'm a master in my own right. You're making a huge mistake in this. When I find you—"

He cut her off with a laugh. "Find me? My dear lady," – and the word came out as a sneer not a title– "you should have a care when you leave tonight. Your name was added to the roster of known villains just this morn, and you will be watched."

The line went dead, and she had to count to ten before she trusted herself to lower the handset to the cradle. Even that was a struggle. As soon the phone touched the body of the phone, it rang again. The small scream that escaped her mouth had her temper flare higher. With a snap of her name, she answered the phone before it rang again.

"Valda La Rue, you're hereby informed that in five days' time you will be removed from the home in which you now reside. The other properties of your mate, one Phillip La Rue, will also be cleaned of all personal items that are deemed as yours and not the estate. These items will not include any cash, jewelry, gems or stones, precious or otherwise, as well as nothing with a value of over one hundred dollars should be taken from the home. I'm to inform you as well that—"

"You cannot expect me to survive without money. How will I purchase a home suitable to my lifestyle as well as those that work for me? Would you have me throw them to the streets? I'm just a poor woman who's lost her mate." She heard him shuffle papers as she sniffled expertly, and was ready for him to tell her he'd cut her some slack. "You cannot do this to me, I'm all alone."

"Your mate was killed over a week ago, and at that time you were informed that you may have to leave the house. You were also informed by courier that this was something that may occur and that you should prepare your household." He laughed slightly. "Your servants will be able to stay on with the new master, and it seems they will have a better time of it than you."

Valda slammed the phone down to more of his laughter. She was going to hunt him down and tear him apart inch by inch. Looking around the room at something to throw, she was startled to see her manservant standing just behind her. He handed her an envelope with a short nod.

"Mistress La Rue. This is to inform you that as of high sun on the morning of the twelfth the household will no longer answer to you. We have been offered a job working for the master and his kiss." Then it was signed with the names of each of the people who worked for her, as well as a

print of their name. Like she fucking knew who any of them were. Looking back at the manservant, she glared.

"How long have you known about this?" He told her that he'd been informed the morning her mate had been discovered dead. "And you never thought to tell me this may happen? Where is your loyalty after all this time?"

"My loyalty, as it were, lies with my family, mistress. And you were informed at the same time as we were. We have taken it seriously." He bowed again as he moved to the door. "Mistress, I will tell you that today is the eleventh. When you rise tomorrow night, the house will be devoid of us."

When he closed the door softly behind him, she did pick up the first thing she touched and threw it against the wall. Knowing that the new master would be pissed, she picked up another item, only to have her arm jerked back and the vase taken from her. She turned to look at the man standing behind her. Valda knew true fear in that moment.

"Valda La Rue, I'm Stephan Silva, and I now own your ass."

~~~

Jimmy held Gab under his arm. She'd been snuggled near him since they'd left the restaurant some forty minutes ago. And now she was sleeping soundly and he hated that he'd have to wake her when they got home. Looking down at her sleeping form and then at where her fingers curled around his thigh, he realized he'd never asked her to marry him.

Lifting her chin, he kissed her gently on the mouth, watching her eyes flutter open. When she looked at him and smiled, Jimmy started to get nervous. What if she said no?

"I was just dreaming about you." His cock hardened at her words. "I was thinking about how tiny my house looked with you in it. We should think about finding something bigger for you."

"We could build." She stretched, and his mouth watered at the sight of her nipples peaking under her dress. "You're going to be in a lot of trouble when we get in the house. You're going to be very lucky if that dress makes it to the porch."

"No, don't tear it. It's the first one I've owned that makes me feel so pretty." She ran her hands down the front, and he realized she wasn't being coy, she was being sincere. "Seriously, I'll take it off for you if you don't."

"Will you take it off for me slowly?" She nodded and then smiled a smile that he felt wrap around him. "Peel it from your skin, showing me an inch at a time?"

"I'll roll my stockings off for you as well. Did you know that these are only held up by the muscles in my thighs?" Jimmy whimpered and took a small nip of her shoulder. "And my panties are a small scrap of lace that barely covers anything at all."

"You're playing with fire." She moaned when he bit into her shoulder again. "We're not going to make it home. Hell, we might not even make it to the next stop light."

She lay back on the seat, and he followed her. Rolling her dress up to see what the panties looked like, Jimmy felt his wolf stir. He wanted his mate. But they were neither in a place for him to have her, nor was she ready for him. Jimmy knew that she was still a little frightened of shifting.

Her scent perfumed the air. When he ran his fingers up over her mound, she rolled her hips up to him and he slid his finger under the elastic. Sliding his finger deep inside of her, he could feel her heat as she soaked his hand.

"Come for me." She shook her head, and he took his fingers from her to suckle them clean. "Come for me, baby, so I can taste more of you. I'll make sure no one hears you scream."

She sat up and pushed him back on the seat. "It's my turn to taste you. I want to take your cock into my mouth and have you come down the back of my throat."

Her fingers danced over his cock, and he stilled her hand before speaking. "You're not going to get satisfied that way. I want to give you pleasure first."

"Oh, honey, you have no idea how much pleasure I'm going to get from this." Gab had his belt opened and his pants undone before he could stop her. Or at least try. He was sure he might have, but when she wrapped her hand around his cock, he felt his eyes roll to the back of his head.

Gab scooted to the floor, and he watched her. Christ, she was sex. Not just sexy, though she was that, but simply sex. When her mouth wrapped around his cock's crown, he nearly came up off the seat and cried out. Her mouth was as hot as her pussy had been.

She was everywhere and touching him where he wanted her to. He wanted her to cup his balls, and she took them into her mouth. He'd thought of her licking a path from his root to the tip, and she'd done just that as she sucked and bit hard at him. By the time she wrapped her mouth over him again, he knew he wasn't going to last much longer.

"Baby, I'm not going to be gentle when I come." Her moan made him rock his hips up and down harder, touching the back of her throat with each stroke. Curling his fingers into her hair, he tried to pull her up, and she dug her nails into his thigh hard enough to draw blood. And that's all it took. Jimmy felt the top of his head explode as he came, crying out her name.

When he felt as if he'd been drained, he pulled her head free of him. Christ, she looked dazed. With her lips swollen from his cock, he felt himself stir to life again. Pulling her up, he ripped the panties free of her and growled at her.

"Come over me. Ride me now." He was surprised when she did just what he'd said. His wolf was nearly to the surface, and Jimmy was having a hard time reining him in. By the time she was settled over him, he rolled them to her back and took her hard.

James

"I'm coming." Her scream startled him and he powered into her. Every time he pulled back to slam into her again, she gripped him harder, so much so that when he came inside of her she held him so tightly within her that he ached. Throwing back his head, he howled. Then he leaned down with a snarl and took her throat hard.

Blood filled his mouth as he came for a third time. She came as well, screaming over and over her release. When she bit him, sinking her canines deep into his shoulder, Jimmy felt himself tumble forward, headlong into darkness.

Jimmy knew that he'd only been out for seconds. Her heart was still pounding under his ear, and her breathing was still harsh and erratic. When he looked down at her, Jimmy knew that for as long as he lived, he'd remember her face like this forever. She was his.

"I love you," he whispered to her. Then when she smiled, he said it again, louder this time. "I want to marry you. As soon as it can be arranged. Tomorrow if we can."

"Why?" He sat up and helped her to straighten her clothes. He needed those few extra minutes to answer her. Why indeed. Instead of trying to tell her that he loved her and wanted to spend the rest of his life with her, he pulled out the little box and held it. She looked at it, then scooted back on the seat.

"I'm not sure you're going to believe me," he started, then shook his head. "No, that's not true, you're not going to believe me. I'm not even sure I believe myself. But I do love you. And to me the next step is marriage. It's been quick, this relationship with us. And I should have taken better care in changing you. For that I'm profoundly sorry, but you're my mate. While that alone should be enough to know that I'll never leave or hurt you, I know that it's not. So why do I want to marry you?"

He smiled when she nodded. Then when she opened and closed her mouth twice to speak, he waited. She'd say what she wanted, and he'd be better off simply letting her get there. When she looked at the box again and asked to see the ring, he opened it and showed her.

"It's very lovely." When she reached for it, he didn't assume she was saying yes. He could see her mind working. "I would have picked the same for me. But there's something you should understand before…if I say yes."

"All right." She nodded and handed him back the ring. He was sure she could see the disappointment on his face, but he didn't say anything more but let her say why she was turning him down.

"I will marry you." He smiled, but she put her finger up and he held his breath. "I don't want to have children right away. I won't quit my job or sell the garage. I love working there, and I'm damned good at it."

"And the hunter job? What about it?" He wanted her to do whatever she wanted. Jimmy was sure it wasn't what a pack wolf would do, but he liked to think of himself as different. More of a twenty-first century kind of guy. But if she kept the hunter job, he was working with her.

"I'm going to talk to Stephan about it. I know he asked you to help out, but it's something…I don't get paid for it, and I'm thinking if you want to build, maybe I should take on another job that does." She flushed at him and pointed to the ring. "That's way too expensive for me. I mean it's pretty and all and I really like it, but we need a bigger house, and I—" He cut her off by putting his hand over her mouth.

"I should probably tell you that you don't ever have to work if you don't want to. And that's not to say that you have to sell the garage, but I've done really well for myself and I rarely spent any of it. Well, that's not true. I've never spent any of it." She nodded. "Would you like to know how much we have?"

"No. Yes." She grinned. "Is there enough for us to have a bigger bed?" He pulled her to him and straddled her over his lap. He knew they were getting close to their home, but he wanted this settled before they left the limo. Pulling out the ring, he slipped it over her finger to the first knuckle.

"Say yes." She nodded. "No, you have to say yes. I want to hear you say the words. Like, 'I love you, Jimmy and will marry you tomorrow.' That would be very nice."

"I can't lie to you." He nodded and kissed her mouth as she slid the ring home. When he lifted his head she put her forehead to his. "But I will marry you tomorrow if you want."

It was better than he'd hoped for, and he kissed her again. When the limo stopped, he set her on the seat beside him and got out. Helping her out, he waited for her to stand before picking her up into his arms and carrying her to the house. It was going to be a very short night as far as he was concerned.

Chapter 8

It was nearly ten before she got around to opening the garage. She was under one of the most abused cars she'd ever seen when she saw a pair of expensive shoes in her line of vision. Gab started to tell the woman that she'd be out in a few minutes when she spoke. Gab wanted to tell her to go away.

"I've just left your house. I had hoped ye'd still be there basking in the warmth of your future husband." Gab rolled her eyes at Kennedy as she continued. "But here you be oily and dirty under a *feithicil*. A vehicle I mean."

"You're pissed off because I'm working or that you didn't catch us in the act of fucking around." Kennedy laughed and so did Gab. She slid her creeper out from under the car to see not only Kennedy but Summer as well. "I'm sorry. She didn't say she wasn't alone."

"It's fine. She had it coming, and as I'm never able to come back with a quick quip, it's nice to see that someone can." She rolled her wheelchair to the workbench and picked up a tool. "I suppose you have a name for each of these things?"

"I do. That's a gear puller. And it does just what its name implies." When she put it back on the bench, Gab stood up and walked over to her. "You didn't come here for a lesson in tools or my lack of manners when there is someone respectable in the place. And coming here with Kennedy, I can only assume it's not good."

"Why would you think that?" Gab shrugged at Summer. "I would also like to point out that your mother is coming too. She said it had been a long while since the two of you had done lunch and she wanted to come along when Kennedy and I kidnapped you."

"I don't have time today. I got a late start, and then there's the simple fact that I'm dirty and smell like old engine cleaner." She pulled her shirt out and showed it to her. "I also have a cut on my leg that needs looked at, and there is no time for it either."

"Where's Jimmy?" Gab looked at Kennedy when she asked her sharply. There was something there, a tone she didn't care for, but before she could ask Kennedy what was wrong, she was suddenly standing right next to her. "Did you know that a vampire has been here as recently as ten minutes ago?"

Gab looked around the room and then back at Kennedy. She might have teased the woman a little but she could hear the fear in her voice as well. Instead she answered her question.

"It was Doug. He works for me. And yes, I'm aware he's a vampire, but only a partial one. I guess you guys have a name for them, but to me he's just plain Doug. He brings me files from Stephan when he wants a job done." Kennedy looked around and saw the file on the bench. When she moved toward it, Gab stopped her. "There are crime scene pictures in there. Not the usual ones either, but pictures of destruction that only a supernatural can make."

"How badly?" Gab didn't move, didn't blink at Kennedy, but did release her. "You're still working for him then?"

"I haven't decided. And when I do, you'll not be the first person I call. Not that I'm trying to be rude or anything, but it's really none of your fucking business."

Summer laughed and then coughed when Kennedy looked over at her. When the younger woman looked at her,

Gab could see the struggle. *She wanted to laugh too but didn't want to let Summer off the hook just yet*, Gab thought. Then she shivered and looked back at the file.

"Can I see them?" Gab wanted to tell her no. She wanted to tell her that she'd been sickened by the pictures within and she'd seen a lot of bad things happen to a good many people. When she released her, Kennedy went to the bench and picked it up. Gab knew just what she'd seen.

"I think he killed the child first. It looks like she opened the door. And like a bastard the vamp asked her to let him in. It was all he needed for him and his buddies to do that. Thankfully, she was dead before she hit the floor." Gab watched Kennedy as she looked at the next photo. "The mother wasn't so lucky. He raped her. I don't know if all of them did or not, but as there is only one set of marks on her throat, I think it was just the one. But there were three others in the house that night. The father was in the living room when the mother was murdered. He was killed on his way to her."

"Are there more children in the house?" When she didn't answer Kennedy, she turned to her and asked again. Gab nodded. "Did they do the same to them that they did the child at the door?"

"No. Worse. They...they toyed with them for several hours before they finally ended their lives. I don't know how long, but I will." Kennedy put down the file without looking at the other twelve photos. Gab wished she could do the same, but she'd seen them all. "Are you going to tell me that this is too dangerous for me? That I should just quit now?"

Kennedy turned to her. "Can you find them? Will you kill them for what they did to this family?"

"Yes." Kennedy nodded but continued to stare at her. "You're not going to try and make me stop this?"

"Nay, I'm not. Even if I had the power to tell ye no, we both know that ye'd do it anyway." Gab nodded. "I am hoping you'll take Jimmy with you. I don't know how ye work, nor do I fully understand what ye do other than kill rogues, but I'm for someone taking out the monsters that did this. If I knew I'd help ye as well."

"You're Irish? It comes out stronger when you're upset." Kennedy nodded at her just as Gab's parents' rental pulled up. "My mother doesn't know about what I do. And I'd just as soon keep it that way. I'm not sure she'll...I don't know if I do or not but I'm not sure she'd understand."

"I think your mother knows a great deal more than you give her credit for, but I won't say anything either." Summer turned to her mom when she walked in. Gab looked at Kennedy who was staring at the file. When she said her name, Kennedy turned to her, but she only nodded.

"Are you sure you can't have lunch with us? I could really...I don't know about you, but I could use something light-hearted now that this is out there." Gab looked at her mom, who looked very hopeful. "It would do us all a world of good I think."

Gab had to find something that wasn't nearly as dirty as the shirt and pants she had on and ended up going with them. She had a shit-ton of stuff to do, and was never going to catch up if she didn't work all week at least ten hours a day. Plus she had to think about doing this latest job. Of course, she had already figured she'd do it, but that didn't mean she'd give in to Stephan so quickly. She looked at her mom when she realized she'd said something.

"I asked you if you're happy. You look it." Gab took her mom's hand and kissed it as she smiled at her. "I'm so happy for you both. This is a beautiful ring."

It was too. He'd told her that he'd seen something like it years ago but had never thought of it as an engagement ring, but when he'd went to speak to the jeweler about buying a ring, this one popped into his mind. He said that the man was excited to do it for him. The diamond alone was unique, but this was amazing.

94

The diamond had been cut into a heart shape, and surrounding it were several smaller rubies. Their brilliance gave the blue diamond a darker hue and made it sparkle perfectly when the sun or light hit it. The band was wide, almost an inch, but it was delicate, and the carving in it was so detailed that when she showed her mom, there was no need for her to tell her what the scene represented. It wasn't until she started talking that Gab thought of her being a wolf.

"It looks like dogs chasing...no, these are wolves, aren't they?" Gab nodded, watching her mom carefully. "I guess that makes sense. Jimmy being a wolf and all."

"So am I." The words slipped out before she could stop them, then once they were out there, she told her everything. "I'm his mate and we're both wolves. He wants to marry me and I will because we're mates, but I don't love him. He says he loves me, but I find that hard to believe. No, that's not true. I find it less and less hard to believe every day." She took a deep breath when her mom laughed.

"You always did babble when you were nervous. But I understand. It's hard taking on another person when you've been on your own so long. And you'll get there. Sooner than you think too." Her mom's food was set in front of her, as were the others. Gab looked down at the ginormous hamburger in front of her and wondered what the hell she'd been thinking when she'd ordered. But when she picked it up and took a bite, she realized that she was starved and scarfed it up, along with the large order of fries. She looked around the table, thinking they'd be staring at her for being such a pig, when she realized they had devoured their burgers as well. The only person with food on their plate was her mom, and she was about half finished.

"You eat like you've had your throat cut." Gab laughed with her mom as she continued. "I suppose being newly engaged to a wolf you'd burn a good deal of calories."

Gab flushed and looked at Kennedy, who was laughing as well. When she winked at her, Gab wasn't sure what to think and stared at her. That made Kennedy laugh harder.

"I have to ask. Why are you named Gabriel? I thought that it was a male's name." Gab flushed, and her mom laughed at Summer's question. "And why Gab? Why not Briel or Riel?"

"I was in a good deal of pain when Gab was born. I'd been in a car accident, you see, and I'd nearly died. Her dad was in another state and I had Rusty with me. I didn't know anyone well enough to leave him with a neighbor, so he came to the hospital with me. On the way there is when we were hit from behind." Summer put her hand over her heart and nodded her mom some encouragement. Gab smiled at them all.

"When the doctor asked me for next of kin to notify, I'd asked him to repeat himself. When he did, I still hadn't any idea what he'd said, but Rusty did. He told them to call my uncle Gabriel. He showed up an hour after my Gab was born. I'd been moved to surgery by then and had no idea what was happening." Her mom looked at her. "Rusty told his uncle that we'd had a boy. Wishful thinking on his part, I think, but Gabriel had been asked to fill out some paperwork in Wiley's absence. He'd thought from what the doctors were telling him that I'd be dead by morning and he was going to take the 'boy' to be raised for his brother. He named the baby for him instead of the girl's name we'd picked out. It wasn't until several months later, when we needed a copy of her birth certificate, that we realized what he'd done. Her name should have been Gabriela, but he'd thought her to be a male."

"So you would have been Gab either way?" Gab nodded at Kennedy. "Well, I'll be *damanta*. That's a good story."

"Yeah, laugh it up there, Kennedy. You know your name isn't much better." Gab looked at the women around the table with her. "I'm glad you talked me into this. I didn't realize how much I need it." They all nodded. *It was good to have friends again*, Gab thought.

~~~

Valda tried her best to think of a good thing to say. She had plenty to say, but she'd been warned three times now that if she didn't have anything positive to contribute, she was to keep her mouth shut. Actually, Stephan had been a good deal less friendly about it, but she got it. When he turned to her, she looked around. There were several others in the room with her, and all of them were staring at her as well. Fuck, she'd missed something again. But when he smiled—and Stephan could do it without it ever reaching his eyes—she knew she was in big trouble.

"I asked you now...five times, I think...what is it you want to see as an improvement to this realm?" Frustration didn't just color his voice but his entire body. "What is it you'd like to see happen?"

The first thing she thought of she nearly said, but she caught herself before she really blew it. She doubted very much he wanted to hear that she'd want him dead and her in his place. He was pissed off enough as it was.

"I've heard that the younger vamps want more freedom." Actually, she'd been trying her best to keep them on a tighter leash, but that wasn't going to win her points. Especially when he found out that she'd been making more vamps nightly despite Stephan's orders to the contrary. "Also they want an allowance to get them by. They can't find work that suits them."

That was her idea. She'd wanted money to train the new ones and no one had come through. It took time out of her busy schedule to make sure that they knew the rules governing them as vamps, so she had started giving each newly made vamp information on where to find the rules and regulations of being a newly turned vampire.

"You're supposed to train your own child. And take the time to make sure that they're well supplied with what they need when you turn them. No money is going to be paid out for newborns. When you make them, you train them. And if I hear that you're not, I'll stake you." Valda said that same thing a hundred times a day and she doubted very much that Stephan wouldn't carry it out if he thought she fucked up. The bastard was going to make her life a living hell, she just knew it.

"What are we supposed to do about the Silver Queen?" Everyone turned to look at the man in the back row. "I mean, she's killing off my children almost as fast as I can turn them. What the fuck is up with that?"

"Why do you suppose she's killing them off?" The man shrugged at Stephan's question. "Could it be that she's taking care of the mess you're making with them? Do you think to see if they are doing anything wrong that would require her to kill your offspring?"

"I think she's just out to make a buck by killing off our families."

Valda looked at Stephan when a low growl emitted from his mouth. The man continued on as if he'd not heard him or simply didn't care. Valda knew the man to be a fool, but she'd never realized how big of one until just then.

It was over even before it began. The man had been ready to stand when suddenly he was no longer there, and in his seat was a pile of ash. Stephan had moved so quickly that no one in the room had seen him. She knew they hadn't seen him move because they were suddenly trying to get away from her and not him as he stood in the back of room. It wasn't until he spoke that they began to understand.

"Get me a list of your children by the next sunset." No one moved to do his bidding until he turned and growled. His eyes had turned as well, and Valda took several steps back, because if he blew, she didn't want to be within an inch of him. "Sunset or face the same consequences he did."

They were gone in seconds. Valda had moved out of the room too and was nearly to her limo when someone touched her arm. She knew the face, just not the name. When the man spoke, she knew that he'd been as horrified at their new master as she'd been.

"I'd like to talk to you about getting rid of Stephan Silva. I think he means to ruin us all, and I, for one, have worked entirely too hard to lose it all to some ass-kicking bastard like him." Neither of them said anything as four of their kind walked by them. The man waited until they were in her limo before he spoke again. "Why aren't you the new master? Your mate was a good man and will be sorely missed."

She had a name suddenly. "Oh, Teddy, you've no idea how much I've suffered these past few months. To be all alone and no one to avenge his death."

"I know, my dear. I know." He took her hand into his and patted it. She smiled at him, trying her best to look like a lost soul. The man took it like she'd meant for him to. "I've tried to talk to Stephan and he's only out for one thing. That's to be the richest master in all the world."

Valda tried to hide her smile. Teddy was already rich, she'd found out. Better off than her...his entire kiss. But the man obviously didn't know that and told her he'd work with her. When he moved to her throat, she shifted on her seat. It had been too long for that as well. She needed a man between her legs now. But he'd only sniffed her throat, and even when she curled her fingers into his hair to hold him to her, he'd pulled back.

"I've a mate." She nodded but didn't care. Before she could reach for him again, he was moving back to the other side of the limo. "I'll help you in any way that I can. We should be able to pick our own master, not have the council do it for—"

"The council? You knew that the council picked him? How long has this been in the works?" Teddy nodded at her and told her five months. "Why didn't anyone think to tell me? I only found out when he came to the house and threw me out."

He'd actually asked her if she needed anything, including money, and then he'd told her that her things would be sent to her rather than her have to pack up such memories. She knew what he was doing. He was making sure she didn't take anything that might belong to him. Valda had told him that she'd be fine on her own and that he wasn't to worry. But now she was. The master was going to kill her when he found out what she'd planned for the Queen. But she'd be gone and Valda would take her punishment. Whatever he thought was the right thing for disobeying him she'd pay it. Gladly. She looked at Teddy when she realized he was speaking.

"...out of the woods one night to find her there. I swear to you if I hadn't seen her I'd say the person telling the story was a liar." She asked him who he was talking about. "The Queen. I saw her. Christ, she is a vision. Dark hair and eyes and a body that would make any male beg."

"Do you know where she came from? Where she went?" He shook his head. "Mother fuck. We have to find her. She's going to ruin everything if we don't."

"Ruin what?" She looked at him for several seconds until he repeated himself. "What is it you think she's going to ruin?"

She had a moment of complete clarity. Valda didn't know why, but she suddenly thought the man worked for Stephan, or worse yet, the Queen. And he was getting information from her to hang her. Or so he thought. When she leaned back in the seat, she asked her driver to take her home. Teddy started to protest.

"I need to get back. My mate you know." No, she told him, she didn't know. "I've a mate that will wonder where I am, what's taking me so long."

"I bet." He looked at the door, then at her. "You didn't tell me what the Silver Queen was going to ruin."

And I won't either, she thought. "Oh, I don't remember now. I sometimes do that when I'm stressed. Don't you?"

"No. No, can't say that I ever have." He tried the door handle and looked at her when it appeared to be locked. "I'd very much like to have you stop this thing so that I can get out. My car is back at the meeting house."

"Do you work for him? The master, do you work for him?" The man started to stutter, but she'd already had her answer. "You do, don't you? You're in league with him and are even now sending him information on what I've said."

"You're insane." She moved toward him and extended her nails. This would be over before he had a chance to tell Stephan a thing. "Let me out right now."

"Gladly." She sliced at his throat and felt his blood spray over her face. Licking up the droplets, she slashed at his throat again and again until she saw his head roll from his shoulder and land in her lap. Picking him up by the hair, she looked him in the eyes and smiled. "Poor baby. Stephan won't hear you now."

When they reached her new home, she told the driver to leave the sunroof and doors open. When she went into the house to watch, the driver did just what she'd told him. By the time the sun was cresting, Valda was dancing around her front hall gleefully as Teddy turned to ash in the sun. For the first time in weeks, since her mate had been murdered, she went to bed smiling.

"One down and two to go. Stephan will be easy, and the Queen…just a matter of time before she, too, is no longer a problem." As soon as she closed her eyes, Valda was dead to the world.

Chapter 9

Kennedy didn't say anything to the room full of shouting people. She watched the couple in the corner who seemed to be in their own little world. Laughing, she supposed they were in a way. She and Samuel could tune everyone and everything out so that they felt as if they were the only two people in the world. But they were needed and this was not going to be solved without their help.

"You should know that I support you." Everyone in the room turned to her when she spoke to Jimmy and Gab. "What? After seeing those pictures, you can't say the same?"

"It's because of those pictures that I think they should get as far away from it as possible." Samuel ran his hand over his face and looked at her as he continued. "You can't possibly know what sort of monster did those things to that family. The amount of horror they put those people through just for the sheer pleasure of it."

"Don't I?" Samuel started to answer her when he snapped his mouth closed. "I understand more than any of you can. And I think they should go out and find the monsters and end them for us all. What would you do, Samuel, if you were the one that had lost all of this? Your family? Children?"

"They're not their family." She shook her head at his statement. Kennedy wasn't pissed that he'd disagreed with her but his reasons for it. "Look. If it were my family I'd want the best looking into this. But that's not important since they know who the people are."

"But someone still has to take them out." Stephan looked at her, then at Samuel as he continued. "Do you want me to send in someone else? Because I will. But I'll tell you now that I'm sending them to their death. Certain death. And it will be beyond what you saw in those pictures. They'll tear them apart slowly, without thought to how much they suffer. Their—"

"We're doing it." They all turned to Jimmy when he stood up, and Kennedy wanted to go and hug him. "We've talked it over all last night and while you guys were deciding what we should do. And we've decided that we're doing it."

"You can't. I won't allow it. Sit down." When Gab stood up after Samuel ordered Jimmy to sit, Kennedy nearly went to stand in front of her mate, but she was being held back. Looking at Stephan, she knew he was doing it to her.

"If she can take him on, maybe he'll back the fuck up." Kennedy looked at the other two, who were within a foot of each other, and back at Stephan before she answered him.

"You think so? I think that he'll hate this no matter what she does to him. But it might be fun to watch her try." Kennedy felt the anger from Samuel and had to calm her lion. She wanted to protect her mate.

"Okay, first you should know that I barely take orders from my parents, and you? You are not my parent. Secondly...secondly, you have no say over what I do. In the event you didn't notice, I'm an adult. And as—"

"Then fucking act like it," Samuel cut Gab off. "What the hell are you going to do if you get killed? And I swear to Christ if you give me a flippant answer I'll show you what I can do." Samuel's lion ran along his skin, and Kennedy watched his body seem to expand. "I'm not fucking with you."

"Neither am I." Just as Samuel reached for Gab to no doubt show her how big and strong he was, she hit him. It was a simple punch to his nose, but it was apparently all she needed. When he staggered back slightly, she moved in and flipped him to the floor and onto his chest. Before he was able to throw her off, Gab had him all twisted up in a pretzel. His legs were crossed, and she was leaning on one of them, and his arms were held up behind his neck. The harder he struggled, the more he seemed to be pressed into the floor. He stilled when Gab pressed something into his spine.

"You move and I'll cut you right here. And I know this place that will sever your spine because I've been trained to know. Just like I've been training Jimmy. Just like you should be training your own men." Kennedy felt herself being released, but she didn't move. In actuality she was sort of afraid to. If she startled the girl, she might really hurt her mate.

"Let him go." Kennedy looked at Jimmy when he spoke softly to Gab. "Honey, let him go so that no one else gets hurt."

Gab moved back but she held her hand to his back until she was standing. When she moved back, it was far enough away that unless he leapt at her, Samuel was not going to touch the girl. Kennedy looked at Stephan. He looked as shocked as the rest of them did.

"I can assume you didn't have anything to do with this training." Glaze-eyed, he looked at her and shook his head. "I didn't think so. You didn't know she was able to protect herself like this, and we can only assume that she can do a great deal more."

Kennedy looked at Gab. She looked…Kennedy wanted to say she looked bigger, but that wasn't it. She looked confident. And pissed. Smiling, she stood up and walked slowly to Samuel to help him up. He let her, but she was sure he wasn't happy about it.

"Where?" Gab glanced at Stephan before looking at Samuel again when he continued. "Where did you learn to fight like that? I'm guessing it was military or police."

"Both actually. I knew a couple of people and asked to be helped out. They thought I had an abusive spouse. I suppose the bruises from each of their sessions helped put that thought there, and I didn't change it."

Samuel walked toward her, and Kennedy had to hand it to the girl, she didn't flinch. "You're not going to back down from this, are you?"

"No. Would you?" Samuel shook his head at her question. "Then why should I be any different? Is it because I'm a female?"

"Yes." Gab snorted at him. "We're told from birth that we're to protect our females. Even if some of them are too stubborn to accept that protection, we're still going to do it. And I'm sure that Jimmy as a wolf is taught the same."

Jimmy nodded and put his arm around Gab. "We are. But recently I've discovered that it's stupid to think that just because I'm a male and bigger that she's any less able to protect me than I am her."

Kennedy moved to the big wolf. He'd had something change his mind and she thought it was the woman beside him. When Kennedy asked permission to hug him, he looked to Gab. These two, Kennedy thought, were going to be the model of how to be a couple.

The hug was quick. Samuel didn't like her touching other males any more than she liked him touching females. When they parted, Samuel looked at the others in the room. He was no happier than he'd been before being handed his ass, but she knew that he'd made the decision to back off.

"I can't stop them, so I might as well help. What do you need from me?" Samuel turned to Gab when she cleared her throat. "You have something to say?"

"I do. You can't help us. I mean, you can't go on the hunt with us. I can smell you." She looked at Stephan, then back at Samuel. "I can smell you now, and you smell like a lion. Not badly, I suppose, but if I can smell you, then they

106

can. You can't smell me. He did that to me. And Jimmy, I guess."

"Then he can do it to me." This time Stephan cleared his throat, and Samuel turned to him. "Do I need to get some cough drops or lozenges?"

"I can't have you going even if I could take your scent away." Kennedy nearly laughed when Samuel cocked a brow. "I need you here. Something might…there might be a problem with this and I need a witness."

"A witness? Dare I ask you why?" Stephan shook his head at Samuel. "Okay, so you're going to be here while they're out killing off three vampires that have murdered five people. Are we going to play cards? Watch a movie together? Or did you have something else in mind?"

"Yeah, I do. I need your help with setting up a realm." Kennedy looked at Stephan when he answered Samuel. A realm? Kennedy nearly asked him what the hell that was when Samuel spoke.

"You're the new master." Stephan nodded and Samuel burst out laughing. "Well, that's perfect. I think we will have fun with this. Come on to my study and I'll try not to make too much fun of you."

Kennedy heard Stephan speak again just as the doors closed to the office, and she thought he called Samuel a bastard. She laughed too and looked at Gab and Jimmy.

"When do you leave?" They looked at each other, then her. She knew that she wasn't going to like the answer.

"We started hunting last night." *Nope*, Kennedy thought, *not at all*.

~~~

The sun was about an hour from setting when Jimmy and Gab arrived at the nest. To say he was nervous was an understatement. But Gab had been drilling him on what to do for hours, and he was better equipped than he'd thought he would be. He looked at her when she handed him a handful of silver coins. He still had to make himself touch them before he could simply take them by the handfuls.

"Remember what I said." He nodded at her. Talking to each other was something else they'd been practicing. *"You just follow me and don't touch anything."*

"I know." This was not the nest where the killers were. Well, that wasn't entirely true. There were killers here, but not the ones that had murdered the family. This was a test run for him. Something that she'd set up with Stephan.

"I'm going to go in first. If there is more than five, we go somewhere else. Okay?" He nodded again. Taking a deep breath, he let it out slowly and then nodded to her. The door opened without a sound. She'd taken care of that as well with a spray of some kitchen oil in a small plastic spray bottle.

The room was pitch dark. He had a moment to wonder how she'd done this before without her special ability that he'd given her when he'd converted her and decided that he probably didn't want to know. Instead, he moved in her footsteps until they were in the middle of a large room.

Looking around, he wondered briefly if they had the right place. It was clean and looked as if someone had come in recently and dusted. When she put her hand on his chest, a signal that they'd worked out an hour ago, he put his hands in his pockets and pulled out three coins. She said to always have three in the event that he dropped one. It was easier to have it than search for it. Moving to where she pointed, he saw the woman just before he stepped on her.

She lay on the floor on a rug. There was no indication that she was a vampire, but she lay there without a single breath and her heart wasn't beating. When he knelt down to put the coins on her eyelids, he was afraid for a moment that his knees would pop. Something that only happened when he didn't want it to. But he moved down quietly and smoothly.

The first coin he put over her left eye. He didn't know how quickly this worked, but he put the second one on her and started to move. Gab put her hand on his shoulder and told him to finish her.

He opened the vampire's mouth slightly and shivered when he saw her fangs. They looked vicious and like they could tear his throat out without much in the way of effort. Slipping the last coin into her mouth, he moved back. Gab had told him that putting the last coin in their mouths was quicker but also woke the vamp up in pain.

The small whimper was all the sound she made when she reached out blindly for him. Jimmy took another step back when the dying vamp started to thrash on the floor. Jimmy watched as she started to bow up from the rug just as Gab touched his mind again.

"She can't see you or scream. I know it seems really cruel, but there are times when I need to do more than ten in a nest, and this helps me. I can't have one of them coming up behind me when I'm finishing off the rest." He nodded as the woman burst into a cloud of ash. *"It works so long as you put the coin in the mouth last. Otherwise they can see you when they reach for you."*

There were two more of the ones they needed in the house. One of them was sleeping alone; the other had a man curled next to him. There were no warrants for the naked man, so she went to the killer and took care of him by herself. While Jimmy watched, she killed the man where he lay without disturbing the other man. Christ, he would have gotten them both killed had he done it. As they moved around the house looking for the others, he reached out to her.

"I need a gun." She turned to look at him. *"I know that I don't really need one, but I need to feel its weight on my person. It's something I just need."*

She nodded and turned back to go toward the opposite door he was going to go into. When she answered him, he thought she would make fun of him, but she'd apparently taken his need very seriously.

"I know this witch. She can help you with that." He started to tell her that he didn't want a spell but an actual gun when she continued. *"It's call the Art of Tat. It's very old and has helped this guy I know a few times. I actually have one myself."*

"I can't tat." She told him that he could get one of these. *"What is it exactly? Something that will protect me?"*

"No. She uses her magic as she puts a tat on your body. My buddy has some silver blades put onto her back. I think she has a couple more, but I'm not asking her. Anyway, the tats are alive. In that when you need a gun or anything she puts on you, it's a part of you forever. I'll take you to her when we have some time."

He tried to wrap his mind around what she was saying when he came across another vamp. This one was young. Jimmy would bet that she was only about twelve when she'd been changed. He asked Gab what to do.

"She's on our list for tomorrow night. Kill her now or tomorrow, it's up to you." He was sort of grateful that she didn't tell him she'd do it and disappointed at the same time. He didn't want to kill a child but knew that if she was on their list, then she'd done something to put her there. Reaching into his pocket, he took out three coins and laid two of them on her eyes. He was ready to slip the last one into her mouth when she moved.

Jimmy felt sweat bead on his forehead as he took a step back. When something rocked on the dresser he bumped into, he closed his eyes only to open them again quickly. If he wasn't paying attention, he'd get them both killed. As soon as the vamp reached for him, he knew that she was going to scream. Pulling her lip down, he shoved the last coin into her mouth and moved out of the way of her hand. But she'd caught him on the leg, and he felt his blood pour from the wound.

"Don't move." He stilled where he was when Gab spoke from just behind him. *"The others are dead, but we don't want to wake the man in the bed."*

The vampire bowed up off the bed and looked around. Then her mouth opened wide as if in a scream and he could see what damage he'd done to her. Most of her front teeth were falling out and her fangs were bleeding. When he saw what was left of her tongue, he knew that she'd not make a sound. There was barely enough there to rub along her teeth, much less try to form a sound. In seconds she was gone.

Jimmy followed Gab out of the house. He needed air and he needed it badly. When he looked up at her, he tried to think what she was saying. Finally, she slapped him, knocking him to the dirt.

"Are you okay?" He nodded. "I don't think you are. I need for you to take deep calming breaths and—"

Jimmy stood up and pulled her to him. What he needed right now was her, and she was going to give it to him. As soon as his mouth touched hers, she came alive with need. They were tearing at each other's clothes even as he took her to the ground. Christ, he needed to fuck her right now.

Gab didn't fight him, for which he was glad. He didn't want to hurt her, and he would have if she'd tried to stop him. But when he slammed his cock deep into her, she cried out and he stilled above her.

"I'm sorry, but I need this." She nodded and pulled him to her mouth. When she kissed him softly, he felt his body relax and he moved in and out of her slowly. As his climax began to build, he moved his mouth along her throat to her shoulder. As soon as he bit her, she tightened around him and sank her teeth into his shoulder as well.

Jimmy started to pound into her again, the need to mark her overwhelming. As soon as he felt his own release pour over him, he lifted his head from her still-bleeding wound and roared out his release. Christ, she was his.

Dropping over her, he licked the wound closed and lay over her. When she giggled, he lifted his head and looked down at her.

"If you need to do this every time we go out, we're going to have to pack some more clothes." He moved the bit of hair that was soaked with sweat from her forehead as she continued. "You're okay now?"

"No. I'm not sure I ever will be again." He grinned. "Oh, you mean about the job. Yes, I'm fine with what we did. I knew it was going to be rough, but having you here to help me relax after really helps."

"Glad I could be of service." She looked away from him as she continued. "I can't make my wolf come to me."

Jimmy nodded. When he'd taken her to the woods last night to play, she'd been unable to call her wolf to her. He'd tried to tell her she would come, and the harder she tried, the more the wolf would shy away from her. The wolf needed to get settled, too, he'd told Gab, but she was still no less frustrated.

"You're going to have to show me something when we get back home." She looked at him then. "This witch? I'd like to see what she does when she tat's a person."

He knew that the change of subject wasn't giving her the answers she wanted, but he figured if she let it go, the easier her wolf would come. At least he hoped so. When she moved her head to the right, he saw three little silver stars there.

"How does it work?" She moved to show him that they went up behind her ear to her hairline, and he ran his finger over one. "I don't feel anything. Are you sure they work?"

She put her finger over the first one and pulled her hand back. There in her palm was a silver star. He looked where she'd taken it and then at her face. There was nothing there. Not a mark, nor a scar, yet the star was right there.

"You can have her stack them. I was going to get more of them put in, but I got hurt and met you." He nodded,

112

understanding what she was saying but still having a hard time wrapping his head around it. "If you want, I can take you to her today. It hurts, fucking hurts, actually, but it's over with in one day. Less if you want something she's done before."

"And she can give me a gun?" Gab nodded. "Then we should get going. I have to see Samuel at noon where we're building our house." As they approached their car, he laughed when they got there. Sitting on top of it was a duffle bag, and inside were changes of clothes. He'd have to thank whoever did this for them. This was much better than sitting on leather seats naked.

Chapter 10

Valda walked around the room. She was pissed, of course, but more than that, she was curious too. Whoever had come in here hadn't been the Queen. She'd stake her life on it. There was something very unprofessional about this kill.

"What do you think?" She turned to look at the man who she'd partnered with last night. "The Queen has struck again, hasn't she?"

"Sort of." She walked to the bed where the ashes still lay. They were of a woman she'd turned only last weekend and now she was dead, but she'd not died easily like the others had. This baby had suffered a great deal, Valda had felt it. "The others yes. I can see that. I did have my doubts on the first one we came across, but now that I see this, I can see that this is the work of someone else."

When she stood near the bed, she sniffed the air. She had no idea why she even tried anymore, but she found that she needed to. Everyone knew that the Queen left no scent. But this time Valda did smell something. Leaning down, she found a small drop of blood. Taking it to her nose, she sniffed.

"Wolf." She nearly leapt from the tiny drop but remembered at the last moment that the man with her must fear her. And one thing Valda did not need was someone who knew her secret. "A wolf was here when she died. I would guess that he's healed by now, but one was close enough to the baby to let her touch him."

Valda put the small smear onto her tongue and savored it. She may be terrified of them, but she loved their taste. And now she had his taste. Finding him would be no problem. Closing her eyes, she tried to find the man and came up with several locations. It seemed that the wolf had been moving a lot in the past few hours. When she felt him at the house of the lion, she knew she had him. Standing, she looked at Devon.

"We're going to pay a visit to the lion. I think he might have some information that I want." Valda moved out of the house and started to move toward the house when Devon spoke.

"I've heard rumors about the lion. It's said that he can control all animals and that his pack is filled with them." Valda rolled her eyes and he smiled. "I said it was a rumor; I didn't say I believed it."

"I have heard the same thing. More than likely they are rumors he's spread on his own." She crossed her arms over her chest and glared at him. "Are you going to be a pussy or are you coming with me?"

He pulled her to him and kissed her. She liked it rough and over the years had gotten really good at finding herself partners that liked to take the pain she dished out. Her mate had never been into it but didn't care if she found what she needed elsewhere so long as he could mark her when she returned. But Devon liked it hardcore rough. And Valda had discovered that she was for the first time in a century having climaxes again.

"I told you not to order me around. I'm not one of your minions." She nodded and whimpered when he tore at her throat. The bite had her nearly to a climax just that quickly. When he lifted her head, she saw the blood on his mouth and wanted to lick it away, but he nearly tossed her to the ground. "When we get back I want you naked on my bed and being serviced by one of the minions you have hanging around. But you'd better not climax with him. That's just for me."

"Okay." She moved to stand, but he took a menacing step toward her. Before she could stop herself, she cried out with a small yet powerful orgasm. She looked up at him when he growled.

"Stand up." She did so only to be knocked back down. When he lifted her ass up and tore off her skirt and panties, she stood bent over, panting, waiting. "You're not going to like this...then again, you well might."

His cock slammed into her ass so hard that she screamed with the pain of it. There was no begging him to stop or let her get used to him first because he took her hard over and over. She felt his hand at her hair. She cried out again when he yanked her head up. "Come and I'll kill you."

Her body reacted to his command like he'd more than likely wanted it too. As soon as he pinched her clit hard enough for her to see stars, she felt him bite down into her shoulder. Even as she cried out, she could feel herself getting wetter. And when he lifted his head from her throat, she knew that what he did next was going to throw her over the edge. Christ, he was going to kill her. But she hit the dirt instead and lay there trying to keep herself from having the best orgasm of her life as she just knew it would be.

"Home now and let some asshole fuck you until I get there. Come or not, I could care less, but you'd better be ready for me." She nodded and stood up, making sure she was at least not within reaching distance of him. "I'll be there with my cock in hand and you'd better be wet and ready."

By the time she made it to the house, Valda was trembling with need. There was a woman in her room when she got there, and she moved up behind her and tossed her to the bed. Right now she'd take anyone.

"Eat me." The woman had been clearing her room, but Valda's compulsion was too much for her to resist. As soon as the woman put her tongue on her pussy, Valda came screaming. Three of her minions, as Devon called them, came into the room with their guns drawn. Valda licked her lips and told them to strip.

By the time Devon retuned some three hours later, Valda had killed the woman and one of the men. The other two were standing over her masturbating and she was fingering her pussy as hard as she could. Devon moved up the bed where she lay, lifted her ass up, and pulled her over his cock. The two men never stopped what they were doing.

"Come here." One of the men moved up behind her and his cock was near her mouth. When she licked it, Devon told her to stop. "This is mine. I'm going to suck him off while you do the other. And when we're done, I'm going to fuck you until you bleed."

The cock was shoved into her mouth before she could tell the man to come to her. She wanted to watch Devon suck the other man off, but she was enjoying her own too much to turn to see him. When the man came down her throat, crying out over and over that he was coming, she nipped his cock hard enough to draw blood and fed from him as he stood there. Hearing the man being sucked beside her, she turned in time to see Devon taking the man as deep as he could and fucking his ass.

She felt her pussy tighten as she wrapped her legs around Devon. She rode him as Devon did the man he was sucking, hard and fast. The one she'd sucked off came up behind her and start to play with her asshole. When his man came, Devon pulled his mouth free and was sprayed in the face with hot cum. Valda licked him as he took her to the bed, her ass impaled on the cock behind her.

Never had she had so many cocks in her before. Her ass was filled, as was her pussy. The cock in her mouth filled her over and over, and when he came, Valda screamed out her release as Devon bit her again. She was racing toward darkness when she thought of how many times she'd come. This was the best sex she'd ever had.

~~~

It took her nearly three hours to figure out what should have only taken her ten minutes. Gab glared at the men in front of her as she picked up the map and studied the area where she knew the nest was. When she saw something that she'd never seen before, she carefully laid the map down and found a ruler.

"Do you know what a stellation pattern is?" She found the ruler and laid it over the map. She nearly cried out when she realized that this was what she was looking at.

"Yeah." She looked up at Samuel when he answered her. "It's a two-dimensional diagram showing lines where the other face planes intersect on a polyhedron. I paid attention in trig."

"You're right, it is, but it's also something else." She continued to draw out the lines using the nests she'd been going to as points. When she was finished, she turned the map to the others in the room and smiled. "It's also used as a five-point star. And in this case two of them."

The stars were overlapping. The second one was in the center of the larger one and they were the places she'd gone to first. Recently she'd been to three of the five points, as the other two hadn't been assigned to her as yet. When she took the ruler again and measured the center of the smaller star, she frowned and looked at Stephan. He got where it was about the time that Jimmy did.

"That's our house." She nodded at him but continued to watch Stephan. "Christ, it looks like we're the center of all this."

"We are." Stephan still didn't say anything to her but continued to stand there. "Did you know?"

"No." Stephan looked at the map as he continued. "I never even heard of this sort of mapping until it was brought to my attention by one of my snitches. And as much as I hate to admit it, I know just who it is that's doing this. Or at least who is setting up this star."

"What does this star have to do with all of this?" Gab looked at Samuel when no one answered him. "Christ, that doesn't bode well for us, does it?"

"No. As a matter of fact, it doesn't bode well for any super." She moved to the wall of books that she'd seen there a few days ago. Samuel had a vast amount of them in his office and a good deal more in his library. But in here was the one she wanted. She pulled it down and opened it as she made her way back to the desk.

"Legend says that there is a great witch that controls all of the land for all worlds. I don't know if it's true or not, but for purposes of this we'll assume she's real. About five thousand years ago or so she formed this shape. In it she put the hair of every animal she'd ever seen and added some human hair as well. When the spell was cast, it was said that humans could shift into these animals. That is where the first shifter came to be." She found the crudely drawn picture of a woman, bent and old looking, standing over the shape Gab had drawn on the map. In the picture, animals shifting from human to animals poured from the center and moved away. Every animal was there. "Then when someone found out what she'd done, she was punished. It was said that this man, a great man, had told her that she'd only live on the blood of humans and she'd never be able to watch her herbs grow during the day."

"Vampire." Gab nodded at Jimmy. "So this woman, this witch, she invented all the shifters, and because of it, someone got pissed off and turned her into a vamp."

"More than that, he changed her to live forever and a day. Thus meaning that she'd never die no matter what she did, and the sun wouldn't kill her. It was something that I've regretted for my entire life." Everyone turned to Stephan as he continued. "I thought what she'd done was play a god.

Little did I know that someday, very soon afterwards, she'd turn my spell against me."

"You? You did this?" Stephan nodded at Samuel and reached for the book. He flipped through more of the pages until he found another picture. He handed it to Gab.

"Is this the woman who gave you the magic?" Gab didn't even bother looking. She knew it was her. It was also the same woman who had tatted Jimmy today. Nodding, she moved to the chair to try and think. "Does she know who you work for?"

"No. I don't think so. For as much as she's done for me, I doubt it. She helped Jimmy out as well." Samuel moved to stand in front of Stephan and Gab moved to protect him. She had no idea why, but she had a feeling that Stephan could fix this. Or at least fix some of it.

"You overgrown, pompous ass. What the fuck were you thinking pissing off a witch?" Samuel started to reach for the vamp when he was suddenly knocked back. No one moved, but the tension level in the room tripled. "What the fuck was that?"

"It wasn't me." Everyone looked at her as Stephan raised a brow at her. When she shook her head, she looked around the room to see what might be there with them.

She started to fade into the room gently. Then when she saw that she had everyone's attention, the witch became solid. She stood there as if she'd not just caused a grown lion to nearly be killed when he'd been thrown hard against the wall.

"Hello, Stephan Silva. It's been a long time." When the witch turned to her and bowed, she spoke to her as though she'd known something all along and was thrilled she'd just figured it out. "I knew the moment I saw you that you'd be doing great things. Saving my creations is what you were sent here for."

"I was sent here? I don't know what you're talking about." Gab moved to stand in front of Jimmy when she looked his way. "You touch him and I'll make sure that you hurt for a long, long while."

"I wouldn't do that. But I thank you for thinking I could." The witch sat down and asked them all to have a seat as well. When no one moved, she laughed. "I shall not harm any of you. Had I wanted to I would simply have done so. I'm only here because there is a threat to my animals. And since you have figured it out, I am free to explain. Am I not Stephan Silva?"

"How did you know?" She shrugged at Stephan's question. "I'm assuming you knew who Gab was all along. You helped her, didn't you?"

"I did. I knew that there would be a need for her soon. Much sooner than I expected, but needed all the same. Do you think I could have something to eat? Sweet would be nice." Gab looked around the room to see if anyone else was startled by the question. That's when she noticed that everyone seemed to be frozen in place…all of them, with the exception of her and Jimmy. "I need you to listen carefully, my child."

"I'm not sure I want you to do whatever it is you're doing to the others. Let them go please." She told her in due time. "If you hurt them I'll—"

"Yes, I understand. And so that you are aware, you and your mate are the only two that will ever be able to set me free from this bond that the young vamp put me in." Gab looked at Stephan and laughed. "He is young compared to me."

Jimmy sat down beside her and the woman. Gab thought about asking her for her name but knew enough about magic to know that she'd not give it to her. So instead she decided to call her "witch."

"What is it you want from us? I'm not going to kill you if that's why you're here."

Witch shook her head and smiled. There was understanding there and a bit of what looked to Gab like pride. It bothered her on several levels that she felt good about the woman having pride in her.

"As much as that appeals to me, I'm needed here. As are you and your mate." She looked at Jimmy. "How is your art coming along? Still painful?"

"Not as bad, thanks. You give me more than I asked for." She nodded again and looked at her. Gab had gotten a weapon put on her as well. She'd gotten a good deal more than she'd asked for as well. "What else did you put on us? The last mark, what was it?"

The tat was covered up with gauze and Gab pulled it off to point to it. The witch had told them that it would make their weaponry so that it never ran out. Gab knew now that it had been a lie, and that whatever was under the gauze, it wasn't as simple as she'd made them believe.

"It's my mark. The vampire that hunts you, they'll never be able to harm you because of it. It will give you everything." Gab started to ask her what that meant, but she continued before she could. "The vampire that you must kill, you will have to fight her in ways that neither of you have had to before. She will use her own magic, and once she or the man who will tell her how to use it unleashes, the world will never be the same. Black magic will reign. You need to kill her before she is fully aware of what she can do."

"I don't like this." Gab agreed with him, but Jimmy stood up to pace and she watched him, wondering what else the woman had done to them. "You're telling us that the man we're to fight is.... Do you think you can do something with the people popsicles? They're starting to creep me out."

They were suddenly in a room that had to be something out of one of those high end magazines. Gab was sitting in a chair that felt like it molded around her body and held her. The room too. It felt like something she'd pick out. The warm colors, the soft textures. She even liked the painting over the massive fireplace. She turned to the witch and watched her.

"If I asked you where we are, would you tell me?" The witch smiled and handed her a cup of tea. Up until that moment there had been nothing on the small table. Now it was filled with a teapot, cups, and a large tray of cookies and tiny cakes.

"You must understand that the vampire you are chasing knows nothing of what she is. All she is aware of is that she's strong. Not just in strength but with her ability to get others to see her way. She believes herself to be persuasive, but it is her gift. The kind that all vampires are given." Gab knew about that. Stephan had told her that with age you also acquired a few more, but he'd never told her what his were. She supposed that was the point. She looked at Jimmy when he cleared his throat before speaking.

"This mark? Will she know what it is?" The witch shook her head. "But you expect us to believe it will keep us safe."

The knife came out of nowhere and was sailing toward his chest in seconds. Before Gab could move to take it, it stopped in mid-flight and dropped to the floor. Both she and Jimmy stared at it before looking at the witch.

"Shall we try a gun next?" Both of them told her no. "Then we are to assume I am correct. The only thing it will not save you from is a bite. I'm sorry for that, but there is no way I can take away what sustains me. For that you'd need someone stronger than what I am, and there is no one as yet."

Gab didn't like the "as yet" comment but let it go when something else occurred to her. "You said that the woman we're chasing doesn't know what she is. Do you? And this man, what part does he play in all this?"

"I do. She is going to be the most powerful vampire in the world. She will command armies of her minions to slaughter humans so that they will be less of them and more vampires. Her terror will reign until the world is at a point where humans will hide beneath the earth to survive, only to

124

become a monster worse than what hunts them." The witch smiled, but it wasn't one that would be considered friendly. "That is if she lives. The man? He knows what she is. He has searched for her for decades…more than that, thousand fold. But he has found her and he trains her yet."

"Trains her to do what?" This time when Jimmy spoke he did so with a great deal of anger. Gab reached for his hand and he took it, gripping it hard, making her think that he needed her as a lifeline. She knew the feeling, as she needed him as well.

"To use the magic that I gave her when I converted her. Valda La Rue is my child."

Chapter 11

Jimmy sat very quietly. He wasn't sure, but thought if he had to do anything right now or even think, he just might explode. His mind was a turmoil of information, things that he was sure would haunt him for years. When someone said his name, he looked up. It took him several seconds to focus on the person and what they were saying.

"Are you all right?" He wasn't sure and told Samuel that. "Well, you look like shit. What did she do to you? And for the record, I'm not happy about her using magic on me in my own home."

"Me either." Jimmy looked around and noticed that they were the only ones in the room. He looked at his friend. "Did you murder them all?"

"Not yet." He sat down on the couch across from him. "I sent Gab with Kennedy to get you two some clothes to use for a few days. The witch asked if you could stay here until your home is complete. I hadn't realized that you'd started yours yet."

"I haven't. I don't know what she's talking about. But then I'm pretty sure I know what the rabbit in Alice felt like right about now. But if we could stay here so long as nothing pops out at us, I'd appreciate it." Samuel nodded. "The rest?"

"Stephan has gone to the lower levels with the strict orders to wake him if anything happens. My mom is in the kitchen with the cook making God only knows what for dinner, and the witch left about ten minutes ago. She said she'd return later to speak with me." Samuel handed him a beer as he continued. "Wanna give me a heads up on what she might say to me?"

"We're going to have to kill this vampire before she comes into her power and kills all humans or drives them to the earth to become their own kind of crazy. Oh, and there's this man too, a mage that has to bite the big one, no pun intended, too, so that he can't create more hell. And before I forget this little tidbit, Gab and I have been marked so that no one can kill us unless they bite us. I'm thinking that having to fight vamps, that would have been the one that I would have given me." Jimmy took a long pull on the beer before he continued. "I'm majorly stressed right now."

"I can tell. And I understand from Gab she can't pull her wolf." Jimmy had forgotten about that. He looked up at Samuel, wondering if he could help her. "I can't, before you ask. She's not a lion, and ordering her to shift doesn't work. Besides, with all this other shit going on, I'd be afraid to."

Jimmy nodded. "Her name is Valda La Rue. The witch said that she's unaware of her powers yet, and this guy, which I didn't get a name for, is supposed to train her. I wonder if she's on our lists."

"I would say that's a good bet. If she's going to be trained, she has to start somewhere." Jimmy nodded. He looked up when he heard the door open and saw Gab standing there. She didn't look any less stressed than he did.

"Your mate is going to be murdered if she doesn't back the fuck off." Gab sat down beside him and glared at Samuel as she continued. "I wore the dress. Even loved it, but I draw the line at taking high heel lessons."

"There are high heel lessons?" Jimmy flushed when she glared at him. "Sorry. I'm too stressed to try and figure out your sarcasm. Did you get anything from Stephan?"

"Oh, he was very helpful. He told me that we'd have to see who he was. Like that was going to help us. And when I told him about the woman, he said he knew her. She was pissed because she'd not been given the nod to be the next master. Did you know that vampires have masters?" He told her he did. "I'm guessing that means something to Stephan, this master thing, but not to me. If she's on a list, we have to take her out."

"We will." At least he hoped they would be able to. The whole not being able to be saved from bites bothered him on a lot of levels. "If he knows her, does he know where we can find her?"

She shook her head. "Did you know anything about a construction crew on our land? They called here this morning asking where our water came from. I told them I didn't know and that they'd better wait until I got there before they did anything. He laughed and hung up on me. I was just coming to see if you wanted to go over with me."

Samuel went with them as well. He wasn't sure what the lion would do if things were out of hand, and Jimmy had no doubt that they were going to be, but they piled into his SUV and went over.

To say there was a construction crew was like saying that New York City was a smallish place. There had to be five hundred people moving around the property, and there was already a shell of a house up, as well as what appeared to be a large metal building. They'd only been gone from the place for less than twenty-four hours.

He found the foreman about an hour after they arrived, and searching for him hadn't improved his mood at all. When the man finally came out of the building he'd been in, Jimmy was ready to shift and tear his throat out.

"What the fuck are you doing here? We didn't give anyone permission to start building, much less have this many people doing it." The man smiled and handed him an envelope that had his name on it. "What is this?"

"The person who hired us told me to give you this. We're to have the building done in two weeks. If we do it in less, there's a fat bonus for all of us." Jimmy opened the envelope and saw his and Gab's name. "She said you'd know her."

"I don't." He read down three paragraphs when he got it. "I'm sorry, I guess I do. But I still didn't authorize this."

"I can't quit now. If I do, then I'm going to have to sue you for all we have invested. And with the economy like it is, my men need this work." The guy put out his hand. "Vicente MacIntyre of MacIntyre Construction, but call me Vinnie."

Jimmy took his hand without thinking and felt an immediate and profound connection. Before he could let him go, he heard a voice in his head. Vinnie must have felt it too because he looked dazed.

"Gab will need to connect with him as well. He will be helpful to you and your work." Jimmy knew the witch was directing him, but that didn't stop him from bringing Gab over to shake the man's hand. She wasn't so quiet about the connection.

"What the fuck, Jimmy? I thought you were going to tell me he was quitting. Not connecting to me like this?" She glared at Vinnie. "You're not human."

The man flushed. Jimmy had gotten that he wasn't but not what he was. Vinnie looked around before nodding. Before he could ask him what he was, Samuel spoke.

"Why do you only have two weeks to get this done? Why the rush?" Vinnie handed him a sheaf of papers, and Samuel looked them over. Handing them back to the man, he looked at him and Gab. "They want it done in two weeks because of some sort of shindig that you're hosting. It seems you're going to have to hire some help soon too."

"I'm not having a party. Who the hell said I was?" He handed her the envelope, and she read it. When she looked up, she stared at him, and he could see the fear in her eyes. Before he could ask her what had happened, she shook her head, but she told the man to do what he needed to do. They all walked away. Jimmy needed answers.

"The witch is building this. She's making sure it's all paid for as well." Jimmy nodded. He'd read that too. "Jimmy, it's our payment for doing this. What if we fail?"

"We won't." He pulled her into his arms and looked at Samuel over her head. He looked as worried as he felt. The house alone put a great deal of pressure on them, and then the added bonus of what the witch had told them in the letter.

"What are you not telling me?" Samuel didn't look upset but concerned. They were keeping a great deal from him, but it was time to come clean. He handed him the letter.

After he read it, he put it back in the envelope. "She said that you two are going to be the enforcers for vampires in this area. Did you know that?"

Jimmy shook his head. "I didn't even know that they needed them. I mean, Gab works for them in a way, but as an enforcer? I'm not really sure what they do other than what one does in a pack."

"I'm sure it's the same." Gab looked up at him as she continued. "We're going to do this. I have to believe that, because if I don't, we're so fucked."

He wanted to tell her they'd be fine, but he wasn't so sure either. Instead, he turned and looked at the house. It looked a great deal bigger than even he'd planned. Jimmy just hoped that it had a bigger bedroom than the one they were currently using.

~~~

Devon rose from his slumber and looked around. It was his habit to make sure that all was well before he moved above stairs, and when he felt the movements in the room, he looked in the darkened corners. There sat his own minion.

"What do you want?" The little man cringed but said nothing. "I give you permission to speak."

"They hunt you even now." The words were softly spoken but no less frightening. "They come to you. And for her. She will die by their hand before the next moon change."

In three days. He had three days to make sure that Valda was ready for them. He moved toward his bath to take a shower as he thought of his options. She wasn't ready for the kind of training he had to give her before he unlocked her mind to what she was. When he did, it was going to take a great deal more control than she currently had. Devon tried to think while he scrubbed his body of her. When he came out of the bathroom, the minion had been joined by another. This one dressed him for the day.

"Find the Book of Secrets for me. And bring it to the house. My bitch is going to have to read it before I work with her." The first minion nodded and stood to leave. "I'm not finished yet."

He'd been finished, but he loved to watch them curl into a ball. Fear was a powerful thing, and these creatures were terrified of him. He tried not to think of what they looked like. They were hideous creatures, and there was nothing that he could do to change that.

Most of the time, they were passable. He could ignore the fact that they were ugly, but they stank as well. They smelled of rotting flesh and honey. Devon had no idea why they did, but their stench usually alerted him of their arrival before anything else did. But their face was something else. One eye eerily in the middle of their face and a mouth that was so small he wondered at times how they consumed anything. But he knew for a fact that all they ate was human blood, and very little of it, too. The minions in his household were the ugliest and most vile he could find. And he liked it that way.

"I've changed my mind about the other. Go and get the book." The minion disappeared. Devon looked at the one who had dressed him and dismissed him with a wave of his hand. Devon went to find where Valda was now.

He didn't care for the woman. First of all, her taste in sex was a bit mild for him. Devon had been around for a while, and he had perfected his own style of encounters. She liked it rough, but he liked it bloody. As he made his way to his office, he thought about introducing her to his bedroom as soon as this was over. And it would be over sooner rather than later too.

His phone was ringing when he entered. Devon had never had a cell phone and had decided long ago not to get one. They were annoying little things, chirping at the oddest times, and sometimes when he was searching for prey, the little thing would give away a human's location faster than scent. He smiled when he thought of his latest victim.

She was down in the sublevels now. Thinking about her had his dick harden, and he called a minion to have her brought to him. He might as well have some fun with her before he had to go out. As soon as she entered the room, he could almost taste her again.

"Please let me go. I won't tell anyone what you did to me." He laughed at her. "Please. I'm begging you."

"And you beg so well too. But you might as well get that out of your head right now. You have to know that I'm planning to kill you when I've had my fill of you." She started screaming, and he snapped his fingers. "There will be none of that either."

The silence was wonderful, and he moved to stand in front of her. When he touched her skin, she jerked from him and he pulled her to him. Christ, what was it about this bitch that had him so hard he could hardly think. When he turned her around and bent her over his desk, he looked at the bruises he'd given her already. He'd been rough with her, but not nearly as much as he'd wanted to be. Opening his pants, he freed his cock.

"You're going to take my cock into your ass and come when I command it." She didn't say anything, of course. He'd taken her ability to talk away temporarily. But she did struggle, which was just what he wanted. Slamming his cock deep into her, he felt the tears of her tight muscles and held himself still. If he came too soon, it would lessen his fun. Moving in and out of her, he held her head down with one hand and pulled hard on her clit with the other. She wasn't enjoying this as much as he was.

Licking his fingers, he wet her pussy for him. He did want her to come if for no other reason than to tighten around his cock. When she started to roll her hips against his fingers, he entered her. Now she was wet, and he tried to hold his climax back a little more.

"Come," he told her and felt her body react. There was no way she could not come for him, and he felt his own climax come racing forward. But he wasn't done, not by a long shot. Moving over her, he sank his fangs into her shoulder simply to watch her bleed. Then he pulled from her. Now the fun part. He allowed her to scream, needing that as much as he did the rest now.

Tossing her to the floor, she tried to crawl away. It seemed she knew what he wanted too. Pulling her back to him as he sank to the floor, he spread her legs. There was his prize. Lifting her up so that only her shoulders touched the floor, he sank his fangs into her pussy and closed his eyes. The best place to feed from a female as far as he was concerned. Drinking deeply of her, he listened to her heart beating as her screaming diminished. He wouldn't drink from anyone close to death. It was something that he prided himself on and something he'd been told he could never do. He'd broken almost all the other rules, but this one scared him. When she was as weak as he'd allow her to be, he dropped her to the floor and he stood up, calling for his minion.

"Take her back to the cell. And don't tie her up this time. Give her…give her silverware when you give her her dinner. Maybe she'll think of what I will do on the morrow." He dressed without another thought to the woman and made his way to his car. He was in a much better frame of mind to deal with Valda.

He'd had to wait for her to rise, something that wasn't setting well with him. Devon liked things in neat rows and things to move along his own timeframe. If things didn't work the way he wanted or commanded, then he'd simply kill the person who wasn't compliant and be done with it. Devon seldom didn't get his way. As soon as she entered the room, he slapped her hard enough to knock her to the floor.

"When I come here, you're to make it your priority to be here and ready when I am. If not, you'll pay for it." She nodded and held her mouth. Devon opened his pants. "You'll suck me off while I try to think what your punishment will be."

She was greedy. He could see it in her eyes. When she crawled to him, he had the sudden urge to tell her to forget it, but she licked her lips, and he could almost feel her on his cock. When she had his trousers down around his knees, she sniffed him. Devon waited for her to ask him, but instead, she licked him from root to tip.

"Suck me, not play." Her mouth closed over him quickly and he nearly whimpered. That was the one thing about her he loved. She could give head like no other woman or man he'd ever encountered. Curling his fingers into her hair, he wanted to slow her so that he could relish in what she was doing, but she swallowed him then, and he felt his eyes roll to the back of his head.

Her mouth was hot and wet. And the way her tongue wrapped around him had him thinking she had more than one tongue. Her fangs scraped along his length, and he felt his balls tighten. When she nipped at him, the pain took him over the edge, and he cried out his release. Pumping hard into her mouth, he held her to him, not caring at all if she could take him that deeply or not. Devon pulled back, staggered slightly, and held onto the chair closest to him. When she sat there looking at him as if she were starved, he told her to call a minion.

Watching her feed from the man had his cock jerk to attention again. Valda stared at him as she drank from the man, and Devon knew that if he wanted, he could fuck either of them and Valda would come. The man wrapped his fingers around his hard cock as she drank from him.

"Want him?" Devon shook his head. He did want the naked man, wanted to taste his hard cock, but wouldn't give either of them the satisfaction. When the man came, his cum shooting a foot from him, Devon watched as Valda dropped in front of her meal and sucked him hard. Christ, the man was coming again as Devon watched. Freeing his own cock, he walked up to them. Ordering the man to lay down, he had Valda suck him from that position. Tearing her clothing from her, he took her hard from behind. Watching her service the young man had him coming quick and hard. Devon fell over her and bit into her back. He didn't need to feed, but the need to mark her nearly had him salivating. He sealed the wounds as the man beneath them took his last breath.

"What do you do with them when you kill them?" She shrugged. "There has to be someone who knows. And if they do, how loyal are they to you?"

"Everyone is loyal to me. Or they are killed. I have no use for idiots." She straightened her clothing before continuing. "Speaking of idiots, what are you going to do about Stephan Silva? He's not going to be ordering me around for much longer if you don't take care of him."

"I have a plan." He sat down at her desk because he knew that it irritated her. Moving some of the shit she had on the desk around would piss her off more. Devon was impressed when she said nothing for several minutes.

"We're going to change things up a bit." She frowned but said nothing. "Starting now, you're going to have to learn to control your power."

"I control it just fine." Devon nodded and reached into her mind for the smallest part of her that he could. When he released it over her, she cried out, and three framed pictures fell to the floor. "What the fuck was that?"

"You. And so you know, there is a great deal more of it as well. I need for you to be able to handle it all." He smiled at her, thinking of his plan to have her think that he'd been generous in giving her the magic that she held. "And I'll give you more and more as you learn the lessons I've given you."

She nodded, and he stood up. Right now they had less than forty-eight hours to get her prepared. If she wasn't ready in thirty-six, he was going to release it anyway. If she didn't have it when they came for her, she was as good as dead anyway. Working through most of the night, they both fell into their slumber almost immediately. But Devon woke after an hour and willed himself to his own lair. He never slept somewhere that wasn't his. By the time the moon was high in the sky, he'd figured out what her game plan was, as well as found out the name of the lion. Samuel Payne was soon to be a dead man.

Chapter 12

"Try to think of her with your eyes closed." Gab wanted to punch Jimmy in the nose. He'd been telling her that for the past three days. Every time he saw her, every second she was awake, he was telling her how to call her wolf. The fucking thing just wasn't there.

"I don't think I'm a wolf." Jimmy snorted at her. "You never know. Maybe that doctor was full of shit and all I am is this woman who can kill vamps."

"You're a wolf. I told you, I can smell her." She had smelled his wolf as well, and when he'd shifted for her last night, she knew he was one. But that didn't make hers anything but a figment of her imagination. Or his. She wanted to stomp her foot and tell him to fuck off.

"Why don't we go to the house? We can see how much bigger it is." They'd not been back in two days. She was curious to see how they were going to make it work. There seemed to her to be a lot of extra height on some of those walls. Surely they weren't going to make the sucker that tall. "I need to get a few things out of the house anyway if we're going out tonight."

"I can take you later, but if we're finished here, I have to talk to Samuel. He wants me to look over something for him." She nodded, knowing that Jimmy and Samuel had been friends too for a long time and they valued each other's opinion. Her only problem with them getting together was that left her with Kennedy.

She liked her well enough. Most of the time she had fun with her. And Gab knew that Summer and her own mom had gone shopping and had lunch several times over the past few days. The two of them were plotting something, but Gab didn't care so long as she was left alone. When Jimmy said her name, she looked at him.

"I asked if you wanted to go now or after lunch." She looked at the house before answering him. "Honey?"

"I want to go home." She turned back to him. "Your friends are nice and everything, but I miss just being by myself. I don't mean you, but there are...did you know that Samuel got a call at three this morning? I was so afraid that I made him let me frisk the guy before I'd let him go into the office with him."

"I know. He told me. Samuel said if you didn't take this job, he had one for you as his security." She moved toward the house when he did. "You found where the nest is, didn't you?"

"Yes. I'm going there tonight. You can't come on this one. It's better...don't shake your head at me. I told you that sometimes I would have to hunt on my own. And this is one of those times."

"Not with LaRue out there. I need to keep you safe." She wanted to stab him in the chest but said nothing as he continued. She couldn't figure out why she seemed to be so pissed all the time. Stress, she figured, and tried to think of pleasant thoughts. "You will either let me go or I follow you."

Gab went into the house. She was spoiling for a fight, and when Samuel asked her about her wolf, she leapt at him. It was over almost before it started. He'd pinned her to the wall and held her a foot off the floor. It didn't stop her, however, and he finally had to squeeze her throat until she stilled.

"Let her go." She glanced at Jimmy, whose wolf was started to take his body. "Samuel, I don't want to hurt you, but you have to let her go."

"When she stops trying to kill me." Jimmy growled, and Samuel did as well. When Kennedy stepped into the room, Gab just knew that this was not going to end well for her.

"Let her down, Samuel. I'll have a talk with her." He put her down, but he didn't let her go. "Samuel, I need to speak to her, and you trying to kill her is not going to help me."

Gab started to brush past them to go outside. She wasn't their child, and she refused to be treated like one. Before she could get the door opened, Kennedy was there.

"Move." She shook her head. "I need to get out of here. Just...just let me go to the garage for a few hours and when I come back, I'll talk to you. Right now I feel like I'm going to explode and when I do, the body count will be high."

She didn't think Kennedy was going to let her. But she crossed her arms over her chest and spoke. "You'll come back here? And we'll talk without you trying to take verbal jabs at me?"

"I don't know about that last part. You give as well as you get." Kennedy smiled and stepped to the side. "Thank you."

Gab was getting into her car when she saw Jimmy come out of the house. She wasn't sure if he had planned to come with her or not, but she put the car in reverse and left before he could get off the steps. It was childish, she knew, but she really did need to get away. By the time she got to the garage, she was feeling a great deal better.

The car she'd been working on seemed to call to her, so she lifted the hood and started fiddling with it. By the time she'd figured out what the pinging noise was, she was singing along with the radio. After that, it was a breeze to pull the carburetor out and rebuild it and work on the next item on her mental list. When someone turned off her music, she turned to look at them and pulled the gun she was never without when working there alone.

She didn't know the man standing there, but he did smell familiar. And she did know something about him…he wasn't human, for one thing, and someone had beaten the shit out of him recently. His bloodied lip and black eyes were enough to have her thinking that she hoped the other guy looked worse. He smiled at her gently, and she smiled back.

"I have a message for you." She nodded, never dropping the gun. "Do you suppose you could not point that at me? I've had a really shitty day and that just makes me nervous."

"I don't think so. I don't know who the hell you are or what the fuck you want. So until I feel warm and fuzzy about you, the gun stays." He nodded and moved to her bench. When he sat down at the chair, she moved closer but not to where he could touch her.

"I've a message for you from someone you should know. Samuel Payne." She nodded and reached for Jimmy. His mind was blocked from her, and she tried to contact Samuel. Nothing. Finally she tried Kennedy, only to find her mind in a turmoil.

"Where is he?" He shook his head once and grabbed it before telling her he didn't know. "Then how about you give me the message and I see if I want to let you live."

"My name is Vinnie MacIntyre. You met me a few days ago when you came out to your new home." She nodded, still having no idea what was going on. "I've been…he was there before I could take precautions in getting my magic up. Samuel came by to see if you'd been there. He and I were alone on the site."

"The message." She waited while he stood up. When he reached into his pocket, she stopped him by shoving the gun into his chest. He slowly pulled out his cell phone and handed it to her.

"I don't have one so you'll have to work it." She watched Vinnie as he pressed on the screen and handed it back to her. It was a picture of a man. "Where did you get this? And why was I to get it?"

He shrugged and sat down as he spoke. "He's the man who took your lion. I don't know who he is and he had his *minions,* as he called them, try to kill me. I don't think they figured on me being a little more than just a simple business owner."

"Did he tell you anything?" Vinnie nodded once. "Tell me what happened from the beginning. I would call you an ambulance, but I'm thinking you might not want that."

"I don't, and I thank you for that." He leaned back on the chair and looked at her from his one open eye. "We were walking back to his truck when someone jumped me. I think they thought I was him until he shifted. They must have been prepared for that so they tranqed him up with something. It took a lot too. I think they shot him up at least ten times before he dropped. Then they started on me to find out what I knew about the Silver Queen. I'm assuming that would be you."

"I guess. Why did they take Samuel if they were wanting to know about me?" Again he shrugged and she put the gun away. "I don't fully trust you yet, but I can't think and not trust you too."

"Thanks. I don't know. He asked Samuel if he knew where the Queen was, but he didn't talk. He did kill three of the six before they got him into the van that pulled up ten minutes later. He also managed to hit the vamp too." Vinnie handed her a piece of material. "I'm assuming you can track since you're wolf?"

"You'd think that." When he asked her what she meant, she ignored him for questions of her own. "You say that he's looking for the Queen. Do you think he means to hold Samuel as hostage?"

"That would be my guess. And there's something else you should know. The man who pretends to be a vamp, he's not as powerful as he thinks he is. There might be a little more to him than a normal human, but that's not saying much." She looked at Vinnie when he laughed. "I did mention he wasn't a vamp before, right?"

"No, you didn't. What do you mean? Why would he pretend to be a vamp?" She thought of her own question. "He wants us to think he is because he will be scarier? Stupid moron. Why on earth would I give two shits if he's a vamp or not when I kill him?"

They both stood up when the door opened with a loud crash. Jimmy came rushing into the room and right behind him was Stephan. Both she and Vinnie had pulled their guns. She should have known he'd have one on him.

"They have Samuel." Jimmy came to her and wrapped his arms around her. "I had to see if you were all right. I couldn't get in touch with you."

"I'm fine. You guys remember Vinnie? He was with Samuel when they took him." Stephan walked to the man as she continued. "He said they were looking for the Silver Queen. I'm thinking they'll trade him for me."

When Stephan stepped from in front of Vinnie, he looked as healthy as he'd been at the site two days ago. She wondered if he'd given the man his blood, but didn't dwell on it overly much. Vinnie stood up and stretched, and she suddenly knew what he was.

"A dragon." He winked at her and grinned. "Christ, is no one or nothing what it should be?"

"And why would you think this is not what I should be?" Vinnie sat down, but this time he turned the chair around so that he was resting his arms on the back. "I've a bit of information if you'd like it. First of all, you should know that even though he hunts the Queen, he has no idea that you're now a wolf."

"I'm not." She flushed when he raised a brow. "I can't bring her. She's being…stubborn with me. I guess I smell like a wolf, but I'm not sure I really am one."

"You are." Vinnie pulled out his cell phone again and pressed buttons. In a few seconds he was talking to someone in a language she'd never heard. Sitting down at her desk, she tried to tell herself that this was as real as it got. She was in a room with a vampire, a wolf, and a dragon. Yeppers, she'd fallen down the rabbit hole for sure.

~~~

Samuel felt weighted. He tried to move and discovered that he was chained to the floor. His ankles were raw with it and his wrists were painfully bruised. When he tried to move his head, things blurred for several seconds before righting themselves. Closing his eyes against the darkness of the room, he reached for Kennedy.

"I love you." He could hear the relief in her voice and told her that he loved her as well. *"I'm glad. Now what the fuck were you thinking getting yourself beat to shit and taken away from me? Do you know how much I've been freaking the fuck out? What the hell were you thinking?"*

Samuel laughed. He simply couldn't help it. She was the love of his life, a pain in his ass, and the most wonderful woman in the world. When he heard someone coming, he closed his eyes and answered her. He listened to the men talking on the other side of the door.

"I was thinking only of getting back to you instead of paying attention. But you must listen to me. Tell Gab that she's right about the stellation. I can hear them talking and they are following the pattern because of some ritual that the prick needs to unlock the magic in LaRue." The key to the door made a noise so loud that Samuel winced. He hurried to give her everything he'd heard. *"The middle of the second star is where it's going to take place. She has to destroy whatever is in that area."*

"I will. You stay well. She said to tell you that she's coming, and when she gets there she's rubbing it in your face how she had to save your furry ass." He could feel Kennedy's love. *"You get hurt and I'm going to be really pissed off at you."*

After she reassured him that she'd let Gab know, he told her again that he loved her. After that, he settled down on the floor to try and look as drugged up as he could. It wasn't hard. His body still had enough in it to knock a human into next week. The first two men who came into the room weren't anyone he had scented before. But the third man was.

"You brought him here, why?" The first man spoke and Samuel opened his mouth to try and take more of their smell in. "Did I not tell you to take him to the building? We're going to need to have a sacrifice, and he is going to be it if that Queen doesn't show up to get him."

When August Shiver, a man he'd never thought to hear about again, spoke, Samuel knew that this was not going to end well for him. But then the man was a moron, so his chances of getting out might not be as bad as he thought. Laughing, he wondered what his daddy would say about his son.

"I want him to die slowly. The fucking prick made my dad disown me. How the hell was I supposed to know that Dad would take his advice over mine?" He snorted. "Well, who is getting the last laugh now, jerkwad?"

"You do know that he can't hear you, don't you?" The third man spoke up, and it sounded to Samuel that he'd had about enough of August. "Why don't you go upstairs and wait for Mr. Devon? He will pay you for your information in getting us this man."

He was a dead man. Not him. Samuel figured his chances were going up more and more that he would be, but August was going to be killed, if not as soon as Devon got there, soon after. Samuel wondered briefly who the new

player was. As soon as the door closed behind who Samuel
assumed to be August, the other two men started to talk.

"I don't suppose we can kill the retard before Devon
gets here." The second man laughed. "I have never met a
stupider man in all my life. Did he actually ask you if you
could get Internet on your phone? Doesn't he know that
everyone has Internet? Fucking asshole."

"I was really blown away when he asked if Devon
would consider taking him on as a partner. Yeah, like that's
going to ever happen. The guy is a walking talking idiot and
should be killed before he breeds." *Too late*, Samuel thought
to himself. He'd read that August had gotten another woman
knocked up recently. *That would be two*, he thought.

They talked for a few more minutes and Samuel found
himself drifting in and out again. When he heard one of
them mention the Silver Queen, he tried to focus on what
they were saying. His head was pounding, but he did catch
enough to help them.

"I guess the Queen is supposed to come after this guy.
You think she will?" The other man said he had no idea. "I
hear she's this tough bitch that never bathes. That's what's
supposed to keep anyone from smelling her. I would have
thought that would have helped in finding her anyway, but I
guess not."

"I heard she has no scent. I think that's what it is. She
can go in and out of a den without anyone knowing she was
there. There's this rumor that Miss LaRue has the scent of a
wolf that was helping her. I guess she's about pinpointed
where he is staying. I went with a crew that went to find him
the first time and found this house that looked like a fairytale
house. He swears it wasn't any bigger than his kid's doll
house." While Samuel could agree with the size, Gab was
still his friend.

There was a noise from somewhere high above him.
Samuel waited for the two men with him to say something,
but all he could hear from them was their breathing. It

seemed hours before anyone said a word, and when they did, it wasn't who he'd hoped. The man from the site had come back.

"Well, you seemed to have him all trussed up. Have you heard from his family yet?" Both men said no. "No bother. Once we contact them and let them know that we have him, they'll be calling in the Queen. I'm killing that bitch before it's too late."

"She's gonna come, you think? You think she'll come here and get this guy?" A kick to his foot had him wanting to leap at the man, but Samuel only counted to ten as the man continued. "He doesn't seem all that bad. You took him down all by yourself. We could probably handle him for you."

"I'm certain you cannot. As I have said to you before, things are not always what they seem to be. For instance, did you know that there are shifters in the world?" Again both men told him no. "Well there are. And this man, while he's all doped up looks ordinary enough, he is far from it. He's a lion."

There was a long silence. Then great peals of laughter. One man had told Devon that he was joking and that he had to know there wasn't any such thing. Samuel wanted to get up and shift for him but didn't. There was much to learn from these fools. But he heard something seconds before the room seemed to tighten. Waiting, hardly breathing, Samuel had to fight hard with himself not to look to see what had happened. In seconds he had an idea that both the first men were getting a very up close and personal view of what Devon was talking about.

Screams started almost immediately. Then the smell of blood. Samuel knew when one of the screams was cut off abruptly that the man was dead. After smelling a strong stench of urine, he knew that the second was dead as well. The man in the room simply laughed.

"Ah, Payne. What am I to do with you now?" Samuel didn't move, not sure if the man knew he was awake or not. "Will the Queen come for you? Do you even know who she is? Or even if she's real? These are questions that haunt me. And if she is indeed real, will she die as easily as I need her to?"

There was a soft click like a door sliding into the jamb. When nothing else was forthcoming, Samuel reached around the room to see if he was alone. But he still wasn't sure. Opening his eyes to mere slits, he didn't see anyone. Rolling to his back, he decided that he was indeed all by himself. As suddenly as the thought popped into his head, there were two people in the room with him. Smiling, he looked up at the woman.

"It took you long enough." Gab said something to the effect of him biting her, and he laughed. "No thanks. I'd like to keep my teeth right where they are."

"I'd like to knock a few of them out for you." Gab stepped back and continued talking while Vinnie yanked the chains out of the floor. "You should know that your wife is a pain in the ass, second only to Jimmy. He seems to think that I'm going to get us all killed."

"Are you?" She shrugged. "Nice. You should know that you're right about the stellation. Whatever is going to happen happens in the center of it."

"Yeah, got that from Kennedy too. Along with a list of shit she thinks I'm going to do when—"

A noise in the hall had her shoving him behind her. He nearly told her he could help when he was suddenly standing in his living room with Vinnie wrapped around him. He turned to blast the man when he raised his hands in surrender.

"Her rules, not mine. She said that if anyone comes, you were to be brought here and I was to stay the fuck away." Vinnie stretched his neck muscles. "I don't care for being bossed around by someone who thinks to protect me. I can take care of myself."

"Do you know what she has for a plan?" Samuel looked around the room when no one answered him. "Christ, are you fucking kidding me? She doesn't have one, does she?"

"Just to kill the bad guys at all cost." Jimmy hugged him. "She's going to get herself killed, and I can't fucking help her."

Chapter 13

Gab pressed herself against the wall and waited. This had to be the stupidest thing she'd ever done. Taking a long, deep breath, she let it out just as slowly. Nothing around her moved. And the hall across from her was silent. Terror was her new best friend.

"I can smell you." She nearly screamed when the woman spoke, nearly on top of her. "You smell of sex and human."

When a cold dampness walked by her, she knew the woman had pulled the darkness around her. It was something that Stephan did when he was hiding. Right now she'd give just about anything to hide like that. When the air warmed a little, she turned her head slightly. Gab could just make out the shadowy form about four feet from her.

"I've been hunting you too. Were you aware of that? You've been killing off my children. Not very nice of you." Gab didn't move when she turned suddenly and looked in her direction. The room was nearly pitch black, and the wall behind her was cold. She wondered if the vampire could see her body heat. But when she moved on down the hall, Gab figured she couldn't.

Stephan had told her before she left that she'd not be able to have any silver on her. He'd told her that as a vamp they could smell it before they could a human or any other creature that was near them. What he didn't know was that one of the weapons she'd had put on her body by the witch was a long blade that was made of the purest silver. Gab only hoped that it worked the way she'd told her that it would.

"It will." The voice coming from her left had her jerk. When she looked at the witch standing next to her, she wanted to scream at her. But the stupid woman only grinned. "She can't hear me."

Gab shook her head. This was becoming entirely too much for her. First it had only been Stephan and him being a vampire. She had no idea why the rest of them, all of them, had been harder to handle but it was. And now…well now it was just too fucking much.

"I met a dragon today. He said he knows you." The witch nodded. *"When will this stop? I mean, how many others are there? I don't think I'm going to be able to take much more of this shit."*

"You'll survive." Gab snorted at her. "You will because you are deemed to. As for Vinnie, he will play a part in your life soon. Not a huge one, but he will be useful. And the bear Kaleb? Have you met him as yet?"

She had briefly. Samuel had introduced her once when he'd been leaving and she'd been coming to talk to Kennedy about something. The man was a bear? Fuck. She was going to need a lot of therapy when this was done.

"No, you will not. You are much stronger than you think you are." Gab glared at her. "You will not take that tone with me, young lady. I'm a good deal stronger than you are."

"Like I care. And I didn't have a tone. I just looked at you. But you should know that I don't think I'm going to do this for any of you again. By the way, stop fucking reading my mind." The witch nodded and smiled as if she knew much more than Gab did about this. *"I'm serious. I've had enough of killing for hire too. You can take the house back if you want. I didn't want it anyway."*

But she did, and she was pretty sure that the witch knew it. "There is a saying about a house. Have you ever heard it? It says that a house is somewhere you stay. A home is somewhere you live. Which do you want?"

The vampire was coming back toward them. Gab looked to the witch to tell her to be quiet and found that she'd disappeared. Great, everyone was nice and safe in their little cozy chairs and she was killing vampires.

Putting her hand on the sword that was a part of her skin, she felt it warm beneath her touch. When she ran her finger down the pommel of it, she could feel it pull away from her body and fill her hand. Slightly nervous about what she was about to do, Gab nearly missed what the vampire was saying.

"I have your lion. I'm going to give him to the goddess for a sacrifice. Won't that be a grand gift? A lovely lion to appease her for what I'm going to get." The vamp stopped right in front of her and looked around. Gab smiled when she thought of Samuel being gone. Bitch was going to be pissed when she figured it out. If she got to figure it out. "You're very good at hiding. Or I'm all alone. But I don't think so."

Her hand came out and wrapped around Gab's throat almost in the same second. Grabbing her wrist, Gab felt herself being lifted from the floor as the hand around her throat got tighter and tighter. Reaching for the pommel again, Gab wrapped her hand fully around it and pulled it from her. It lit up the room with its brilliance.

She was dropped as soon as she drew the long sheath of silver back. The vamp backed up but Gab had already started to bring it around. When it cut through the air, both she and the vamp stood there for several seconds before Gab realized that she must have missed. It wasn't until the other woman's head rolled forward that she knew that she'd cut off her head. Another three seconds passed before the body burned to ash, then the head shortly after.

Gab dropped to her knees. Weak with relief, she sat that way for several minutes while she tried to get her heart rate back under control. Christ, she'd just cut someone's head off. And she'd not been nearly killed in the process. It just seemed…well it seemed much too easy.

"Are you hurt?" She shook her head before she realized that Jimmy was talking to her in her mind.

"No. Terrified, sick to my stomach, my heart feels like it's going to pound out of my chest but not hurt. Are you okay?" He told her he was. *"I killed her."*

"I know. Are you ready to come home?" She laughed at him. He was so calm sounding. *"I love you."*

"I think I love you too. I'm sorry if that doesn't sound right but it's been a really fucked up day." She heard him laugh. *"I don't suppose you can send someone to come and get me, could you? Vinnie didn't use a car when he brought me here."*

"Stephan is coming for you. He's talking with someone now about something. I don't know what language he's speaking, but I can tell that someone on the other end is not a very happy person. I think that I might have Stephan teach me a few of what I'm assuming are curse words." Gab stood up as Jimmy continued to talk. *"Samuel said to tell you thanks. He also said that you're going to get your ass kicked by him when you get here."*

"Tell him he's welcome and to fuck off." She made her way through the house looking for some of the others. She stepped over three bodies in the hall that looked like someone tore their throats out. "I wonder if the saying is true about vampires and that when their maker dies they do too."

"It isn't." Gab stopped moving when Stephan suddenly appeared. "I thought I told you to wait until I gave you the signal."

As she'd been telling herself over and over, she'd had enough. Drawing back her fist, she slammed it into Stephan's face as hard as she could. When he staggered back and tripped over the body that lay just behind him, she watched in fascinated horror as he fell back to the ground and landed in the filth.

"I hate you." Suddenly she was standing in a room she didn't know and drew her sword. Then she saw Jimmy standing there with his hands up. "Where the fuck am I now?"

"Our home."

~~~

Jimmy watched her closely. She didn't move from where she'd been dropped but stood there looking at him with her sword still drawn. When she finally blinked, he felt a little better but not completely.

"They finished it today. I was brought here just after you killed Valda." He spoke softly, not wanting to startle her. "I think that this is the only room with furniture in it. I was told by the man downstairs that it would be coming soon."

"It's a really big bedroom." Jimmy nodded and took several small steps toward her. She looked around the room as she put away the sword. "I'm very stressed. I don't suppose there's a bathtub that I could drown in?"

"There is. One big enough for us both to drown in if you'd like." He pointed to the door closest to her. "I think it was designed by someone who liked to bathe or a giant. The room is as big as your old bedroom."

"Do you think we can take a bath together?" She looked lost. He nodded and moved to touch her. As soon as his fingers ran down her arm, she melted against him. He hadn't realized how much he needed this as well. Leading her to the bathroom, he spoke to her. As soon as he entered, he reached into the tub and turned on the water. He'd been told that there was a hot water heater especially for this room, so he knew there was enough hot water for him to fill the tub twice over. He looked at her standing just where he'd left her.

"We need to think of buying furniture. Yours will fit, but it's not nearly enough." He stepped back from her to unbutton her shirt. "I talked to Vinnie...did you know he was a dragon? Anyway, he said that the witch had faeries and gnomes help with the building. Apparently they never sleep and can work much faster than a human or even most shifters can."

He was babbling, and he was pretty sure she knew it. When he peeled her shirt off and dropped it to the floor, he saw that it was covered in blood. Jimmy decided that everything she had was going to be burned. When he turned her around and had her lean onto the counter, she looked at him in the mirror.

"She's dead." He nodded. "I had to kill her now or be killed. Do you think that the witch will be pissed? It was important to her that I try and keep her until we had Devon."

"I'm sure that she'll be more than glad that you didn't let yourself get killed." *And if not*, he thought, he'd make sure she understood that he was glad that his mate chose life over the vampire.

Her boots took some doing. He'd never taken another person's boots off before, and having to unlace them and yank them off was strange. Once he had the first one figured out, the second one wasn't as bad. Then he took off her socks. These too were added to the growing pile.

Pulling her pants down slowly, he felt his cock ache. Looking at her legs, strong and toned, he noticed that she'd been hurt. It wasn't really bad, but would more than likely have needed stiches if she'd been human. Blood had run down her leg and still seeped a little. He would bet any amount of money that she'd not even known it was there. Licking it, he could taste her blood. He looked up at her when she moaned.

She was in the position he'd wanted to take her in for days, sitting high enough up that if he stood, he could take her deep and hard. But looking at her face, he realized she needed him, but not sexually. At least not yet. Standing up, he reached over and turned off the taps. All he had left to take off her was her bra and panties. And there wasn't much of them either.

"Come on." She nodded at him as he helped her slide into the water. He had to take several deep breaths to calm himself when she moaned again. Christ, this wasn't going to be as easy as he'd thought. Stripping down as quickly as he could, he slipped into the tub and moaned himself as he sat opposite of her. It had been years since he'd taken a bath, and he suddenly wondered why he'd ever stopped. Picking up the sponge that had been laid out, he poured some of the bath soap onto it and picked up her foot.

"Why are you way over there?" He looked at her when she spoke. "I just thought that we'd be a lot closer. I mean, like me sitting on your lap closer."

Jimmy felt his mouth water at the thought of her riding him. "You want to sit on my lap? Because if you do, it's not going to be as relaxing as I think you might need."

Gab crawled toward him, smiling. He felt his cock thicken at the look on her face and knew that the moment she settled over him she was going to get the fucking of her life. When she stood up to no doubt sit on him, he leaned toward her pussy and kissed her.

"Jimmy, please help me come." Cupping her ass, he pulled her toward him and licked her hard nubbin that was peaking from her slit. Suckling it hard, he nipped at it gently and then laved his tongue over her. She was hot. Cream filled his mouth as he slid his fingers up her thigh and into her heat. She was riding him now, and he was loving it. When she curled her fingers into his hair, he pulled her closer still and suckled her again. When she cried out, flooding his mouth with her hot juices, he drank from her greedily.

"Ride me." He leaned back as she stepped around his legs. When she was close enough again, he couldn't resist taking another taste of her. Her pussy was so sensitive that when he licked her, she cried out in pleasure. Helping her slide over him by holding his cock, he nearly came when she leaned in and bit his throat. Water sloshed over the edge as she tried to get her rhythm. Jimmy let her, sampling her breasts each time one came close enough for him to taste. As soon as her legs wrapped around his waist, he cupped her ass to help her with her ride.

"I'm going to mark you when you come. I love you. I need to claim you again." She nodded before answering him. Her voice was harsh, lust-filled.

"Yes, please. Please, when you bite me, I come so hard." Standing, he lifted her up and stepped out of the tub. There was no time for playing now, he needed to fuck her. Sitting her on the counter again, he moved her back so that her shoulder rested on the mirror. Taking one pert nipple into his mouth, he sank his teeth into her until he tasted blood. Her scream was enough to take him over the edge with her. As soon as she bit him, Jimmy cried out.

"Mine. You're mine." She nodded. "Say it. Say it while I shoot my cum deep inside you. Say you're mine."

"I'm yours. I'm all yours. Forever, I'm all yours." Her sob told him she was going to come again, and Jimmy took her throat. When she screamed out his name, Jimmy felt as if he was the luckiest man in the world. Coming hard, he held her until he emptied himself inside of her, and his heart began to slow.

He laid her on the bed. Drying her off had been difficult with her falling asleep. But he was having fun, she'd been exhausted, and even though he hadn't counted on it, the bath really had relaxed her. Him, too, if he was honest.

Jimmy heard his phone ringing in the bathroom and went in to answer it, closing the door behind him. He smiled when he saw who it was and waited while Kennedy blasted him for five minutes before she settled down. Apparently, she thought that they should have come to their house as soon as this was over.

"I'm sorry. Well, not really, but you can think I am. She needed a bath and some rest. I just put her to bed." He heard her laugh, but she didn't ask him how he'd relaxed her as he'd thought she would.

"When can we see the two of ye? Samuel is so grateful to be home and all right that he wants to have a dinner *páirtí* in honor of her." Jimmy thought about the dinner that he and Gab were to host in a few days and wondered how they were going to manage it. "Are ye listening to me?"

"Yes. But I don't know what you mean. I know what you said, but not…I'm having a hard time focusing all the sudden. You want us to come over tomorrow night for dinner and we're to behave ourselves. What do you mean?" He was suddenly feeling the stress of the past few days, and wanted nothing more than to fall into bed and sleep.

"I mean no finding a dark corner to make love in." She laughed when he tisked at her. "I mean it. Summer and I have been planning this thing for two weeks, and I'll not have the guests of honor nowhere to be found."

"We'll try our best. But I do remember a time when we were supposed to have dinner together in that nice restaurant and you and Samuel were out of touch. I still don't believe you had a flat tire." She huffed at him. "Seriously, if we have the urge I'll let you know first, deal?"

"Ye most certainly will not. I'm not a pervert, I'll have ye know." He assured her that he did know. "I just want to have a party, and for the two of you to be there." Then she did something that frightened him more than anything he'd seen lately. Kennedy Payne burst into tears.

"I'm sorry." Jimmy told her several more times as she sobbed and sobbed. He felt his heart break in all sorts of places. When she finally told him she was fine, he asked her if she was all right.

"It's this baby thing. I'm so emotional I find meself crying over the dumbest shit. Yesterday I cried at a commercial. Who the fuck cries when a commercial comes on? I don't." She huffed at him again. "And ye tell one soul that I cried and I will tear your dick off and make ye eat it."

"Never. I won't tell a soul." After a few more minutes of her telling him again not to be late, they hung up. Jimmy went downstairs to see if the man who'd been at the front door when he'd gotten there was still around.

"Sire." Jimmy turned when he heard the man talk. "There is all manner of food in the kitchen should you and the missus wish for something to eat. I understand that there was a happening today and she might have missed her meal."

"She more than likely missed a couple of meals." He followed the man into the kitchen. "I don't think I caught your name. I'm James Burger, my...well, my future wife is Gabriel Parker. We go by Jimmy and Gab."

"Milford Peterson, sir. My wife, who will run the house if you see fit, is Nova. She is leasing us a house as we speak." Milford put a bowl of salad in front of him, and Jimmy looked at him. "You do not care for salad, sir?"

"Milford...I can call you Milford, right?" He nodded at him and Jimmy nodded back. "First, who hired you to come here? The witch?"

"She did. She said that we would be working for you until such time that you found someone you wanted. That's why we're leasing a house. The missus and I saw no reason to purchase a house when we may not be here long."

"You'll be here for as long as you wish. If I don't scare you off, that is." Milford raised a brow as he took the salad away. "If the witch hired you, I'm assuming she told you what we were."

"She said that you were not human. I don't believe she said what you might be." He told him wolves. "I see. Then a salad would not be something that you'd like."

"No, not really. And for the record, we have a lot of friends as well. One is a lion, another is a bear. We also have a vampire friend, though I don't think he eats anything." Milford nodded, then grabbed the back of the chair. "Oh, and I think that Gab knows a dragon, though I don't know how much he'll be coming around. We just met him."

"And will these people…will these people be wanting anything…." Milford sat down and took a deep breath before he continued. "I don't believe we've ever worked for a dragon before. Or for that matter, a vampire. Will he be…will the vampire require us to feed him?"

It took him several seconds before he understood what the man was asking him. But before he could assure him that he would not be a meal for anyone, the screaming started. Standing up, he felt his heart pound, and then he ran toward the stairs. He saw Milford moving as well, but he was a good deal ahead of him when he crashed open the bedroom door. Gab was sitting in the middle of the bed, still screaming. Jimmy shifted to protect her. From what, he had no idea, but he was going to kill whatever it was that dared to terrify his mate.

KATHI S. BARTON

Chapter 14

Devon was pissed. He walked the length of the room again. But stepping over the bodies was becoming tedious. And there were a lot of bodies. When someone knocked on his door, he snarled at them to enter. The man standing there looked around and stayed where he was.

"We know where she was killed. At the house." When Devon stepped toward the man, he pulled a gun. "You might be my boss, but I will kill your fucking ass if you come near me."

"She's dead. Fucking dead." Elliot Jennings neither lowered his gun nor came into the room. Not that Devon blamed him. He was still seeing in a haze of red. "I want that fucking Queen now. Where is the lion?"

"Gone too." That nearly put him over the edge. But instead of taking it out on Jennings, Devon picked up his desk and threw it out the window. Nothing was going as planned, and now his only hope of conquering the fucking witch that cursed him was dead. He turned to Jennings.

"I want her found. The Queen, I want her here tonight." Devon waited for him to say something that would allow him to kill him, but he said nothing but only shook his head. "What do you mean no? No, you won't find her, or no, you won't bring her to me?"

"I can't find her. In the event you didn't understand what happened, she killed a powerful vampire, one that had all these powers, and she still managed to take her head. And it's doubtful that Valda was even able to touch her. There is no blood of the Queen's anywhere. As for the lion? Christ, do you know what was done to the chains we had him down with? Broken. Not just that, but whoever released him pulled them out of the fucking floor without so much as a piece of equipment."

"So? She's strong. Wouldn't you think she'd have to be if...?" Devon growled. "I really hate this head shaking shit. Tell me."

"The chains were not put into the floor. They were a part of the floor. When the house was built a century ago, the chain was a part of the foundation. As in, the beginning of it is below the stone embedded into fifty feet of bedrock. The chain wasn't broken, but pulled completely out. Whoever yanked it out isn't just strong, but fucking amazingly over-the-top strong. Stronger than magic strong." Devon didn't believe that for a second. He was strong, stronger than most supers even, but what Jennings was saying was too much.

"What is she?" Jennings didn't answer him, and Devon didn't really expect him to. She wasn't human was all he knew, and she'd fucked him over. Starting to pace again, he got to the window that was now letting rain come in. The desk and all its contents were being picked up by minions. The rain had ruined most of the shit, but he didn't tell them to stop. It was good for them to get a nice soaking. They'd appreciate their cells a good deal better when they went to bed.

"I have a plan." Devon turned to Jennings. "It's not something that is going to keep her alive for you, but it's a plan."

"I need her alive. She has Valda's powerbase and I need it." He turned back to the yard as he continued. "Do whatever necessary to find her for me. Once you do, I'll get her. I'm not concerned with her strength. It's her power I want."

Devon had to have the power. He had to make it his because he was no longer able to sustain himself with what he'd been doing for the past three hundred years. It was no longer an option for him to kill other mages. There were none left to offer him anything that would keep him going. In fact, he had a feeling he was the last of his kind. Turning, he looked at Jennings when he cleared his throat.

"I'm going to need more money for this. I mean, a great deal more than the million you already owe me." Devon nodded, knowing that any amount that the stupid panther wanted wasn't going to be paid to him. He was going to be dead the moment he had the girl. That was if she didn't kill him first.

"I will double your price if you bring her to me alive. I don't care if she's beat to shit, I can let her heal from that, but dead does me no good." Jennings nodded, then smiled. "Yes?"

"I was wondering what you'd give me if I found your witch, too." Devon turned completely around. "She, I found. I'm not sure why she's in this area, but I found her the other day. Her scent is something that I know."

Devon tried to think. He was beyond excited. If he could get the witch that held him, then he could kill her. He didn't know if her spell would continue if she was dead, but he was willing to try. Trying his best not to show his excitement, he nodded once at the panther.

"If you can find her, bring her along too. She might be some fun." In his heart, he knew that the witch was going to give him what he wanted or die. Not that she wouldn't die anyway, but he'd have all he needed with her death.

After Jennings left, he sat down. The witch had taken everything from him. And all he'd gotten in return was immortality. He remembered the first time they'd met and the last time he'd seen her. But he'd heard from her, as recently as a month ago, just when he'd found Valda.

"I will give you what you want, but it will come with a price." He nodded. Being so young and full of himself, he had figured that whatever she'd want was nothing compared to him being able to live forever. "You don't want to hear the conditions?"

"Nope. Just give it to me." She smiled, and he should have known then that details would have been nice, but she walked to him and put out her hand. He had closed his eyes, but opened them quickly when he felt her hand on his heart. Her pulling it out while it still beat had him screaming in both terror and pain.

"Now you belong to me." She put his beating heart into a bag that was suddenly there and smiled at him. "You'll be immortal so long as you never take what is not freely given, give back to the earth ten times what you take, and never drink from the dead."

That last part got his attention. "Drink from the dead? What do you mean 'drink'? You think I'm going to do that?"

"You will if you wish to survive. You'll not be a vampire but close." She put out her hand again, still covered in his blood. "Do you wish to still bargain with me?"

Drinking from people? Being a vampire? He hadn't been sure he could do it. In fact, it was the one thing that nearly had him tell her he'd changed his mind. But in the end, he'd taken the deal and had been touched by her bloodied fingers. When he woke some three days later, he was alone in his home and there was a note from the witch.

"If you break my rules, I will come for you. On the summer solstice after I find that you've reneged on our deal, I will take back what I have given you and give you back your heart. It will no longer work in your body but be dead to you. As dead as you will be."

Devon had broken each of the rules except the last one almost from the very start. The first twenty-four hours he'd stolen a car as well as taken a man's life. The next week he'd found the first mage and had figured out from him that killing one more powerful than himself would afford him all that he'd been. Killing a mage was just like a "get out of jail free" card to people like him, never having to work on the magic but getting it anyway. And he'd destroyed so many acres of fields burying the dead that he'd never be able to pay it all back, even if he had a mind to. But he'd never been punished until recently.

The letter had come just after he'd met Valda. It was addressed to him in his full name. No one had ever known his last name but his family, and they had long since been worm food. And the moment he'd seen the handwriting he knew that he was in trouble, and that the witch had come for her payment.

"It is time for you to die, Devon Robert Anderson." That was all it said. No name, no date, just it was time. Devon shivered when he thought of all he'd done and all he was going to have to pay for. And now that Valda was dead, he had nothing to fight back with. His plan had gone to shit. Devon was going to bring Valda's magic forth. See what of it he could use, then kill her. But he needed the Queen dead.

He'd met a man who'd been searching for Valda. Of course, all he knew about her was that she was a powerful vampire, one that didn't have a clue of her own worth. The mage had told him that when the vamp was found and her power released, she'd be someone to reckon with. Devon made it his priority to find her and help her until such time that he killed her. She would be his. But the rest of the man's words still haunted him.

"The Queen is going to kill the vampire as soon as her magic is fully aware. When she does, the Queen will be the most powerful being in the world. Hell, more than the world, all worlds. It will be for the best, I think. I've heard that she's power hungry, this vampire, and that she will ruin it for the rest of us. I'd just as soon be able to do my bits of magic and be left alone. How about you?"

He'd told the mage that he'd had enough magic and that having more would only be a burden. Lies. It was all lies and he'd killed the mage a week later when he'd found all he could from him. It had been the last easy thing he'd done.

Power was what he'd craved even back then. And the more he thought about the magic and having it, the more he decided that finding the queen, killing her before she did the vampire was the only way to go. But he also had to find the vampire.

It had taken him nearly ten years. He'd kept his eye on the goal and had looked for the Queen at the same time. Finding her had been much harder than he'd ever thought. For one thing, no one knew her name, and another, she never left any clues for him to find her.

And now? Now he had to find the nameless bitch and kill her. Laughing, he thought something else. What if she wasn't even a female at all? What if—and this was the funniest thing he'd thought of in decades—what if she wasn't just a single person but a group of beings set out to end the world of vampire all together? Devon was still laughing bitterly when he went to his lair. He simply had to find her.

~~~

Wiley wandered about the room. It was a lovely home, made more beautiful by the couple living there. He glanced at Jimmy again, wondering for perhaps the hundredth time what ailed the boy. Wiley would bet his last dollar that it had to do with how his little girl looked. She wasn't sleeping well, any fool could see that. Walking to her to have a little talk, Wiley knew it was well past time to ask her a few questions.

"You okay, honey?" She nodded and smiled at him. Sitting next to her like this, Wiley could see that she wasn't fine at all but in a bad place. "You want to talk to your old dad about whatever it is? That man, Jimmy, hurting you?"

"No." She answered him right away, but it didn't ease his mind. He looked over at the boy again and thought that he could see love there, but he'd been around abused women before. He knew the look. "I'm not sleeping well."

"I can see that." He reached for her hand and held it in his. "What's ailing you? You worrying about this here man? The one you're set out to arrest?"

He didn't really understand what she did. He knew that she was a hired gun, sort of, and that Jimmy was going to be her sidekick. Wiley also knew that she was hunting vampires that had gone bad, and that was one of the reasons he and Janice were staying with them instead of at the hotel. Not that he minded too much; there were worse things than living with your little girl in a house that was twice the size of the hotel they'd been staying. And he got to see her every day. He just wished it was under better circumstances.

"That man, Samuel. He said he'd give me a job working here. I'm thinking of taking him up on it. I've been a working stiff all my life, but being here close to you will make it worth whatever job he has for me." The pay was better too. And when Rusty had died, all those bills had come their way. Both he and Janice had had to come out of their golden years to find a job. Not much out there for a man his age.

"I wanted to talk to you about that. Those bills from Rusty? We've had someone look into them, and you're not responsible for them. There was a mistake." She looked at him and then shook her head. "No, that's not right. Someone fucked with you. And Stephan is getting your money back. There is no way that you have to pay a fine for him dying."

He let the f-word slide to get to the point of her statement. "What do you mean 'a fine'? We thought it was for his credit cards and stuff. That man that we talked to said that he had had a debt. It was a fine?"

"He was charging you for his child." Wiley had heard that word before. He asked her what that meant. "The man who turned him. He told Stephan that when Rusty…when he died that whatever money he owed his maker was no longer going to be his, and he thought that his family should make up for it. He'd been doing it to other families as well. Stephan is making him pay it all back. You should get the money soon."

It was a good deal of money, too, he thought. All of their savings had gone to the bills, and it hadn't been a drop in the bucket. Wiley supposed that if you lived forever that you'd mount up some revenue. Relieved that was taken care of, he looked at his daughter. He had an idea that had been bouncing in his head since he'd found out about the letter from Janice. He decided it was time to find out just how smart he was.

"You helped him die, didn't you?" She looked at him sharply, and he knew. "You killed him to help him no longer be the monster he was."

"I don't…." She looked like she was going to get up and leave him, but he put his free hand on her thigh. "I don't know what you're talking about."

"Sure you do. Look at me, Gabriel Parker, and tell me to my face you didn't help your brother out when he asked you to." She looked at him, then away. The tears in her eyes nearly had him backing off, but sure as he was sitting there, he knew that's just what was keeping her up at night.

"He'd called me. The week before he…the week before. There was something wrong, he told me, something that I had to come and help him with. When I got to him, he was…." Gab took a deep breath. "He'd tried to meet the sun. A way for vampires to die, but he'd only been in it long enough to burn himself badly. His body was covered in blisters, and his face…. He looked like he'd been deep fried."

"Could he have been saved?" He had no idea why he thought so, but Wiley had been reading up on lore about them, and he'd thought that if he'd taken some blood, he would been all right again. Then he thought of something. "Did he want to be saved?"

"Rusty didn't want to be saved. He said that he was a monster and didn't want to live. I didn't know it at the time but he'd been changed against his will. They're not allowed to do that...vampires I mean. They have to do so willingly." Gab looked at her hands as she continued. "He told me that he'd killed a woman. He'd not meant to, but he'd bitten her and didn't know how to stop the bleeding. And after he'd...after he'd finished with her, he had to leave the area so he'd not go to jail. It became a pattern, Rusty told me. He would bite someone and they'd die. But he said he couldn't stop. So he wanted to die."

"I can see that." She looked up at him. "You didn't kill your brother, Gab. You saved him."

He could tell she didn't believe him. And why should she? When she opened her mouth, he tried to stop her to explain, but she wasn't having it. Wiley's heart broke for both his children, the one now gone and the one that sat before him grieving.

"I cut his head from his shoulders. I watched as he turned to ash, burned up like wood in a fireplace. How is that saving him? How on earth do you think I felt taking the life of the only person in the world who I loved more than me?" Wiley reached for her, but she stood up. "I killed him as surely as I killed any of those other people. I did it—"

"That's enough." Wiley turned to see the man who spoke. The man, Stephan, he thought his name was, didn't look any happier with Gab than he felt. When he told her to sit, she fought him, but she finally did. "What do you suppose would have happened to say your father or mother had he come to them begging them to kill him? Or anyone for that matter. Do you suppose they would have done it, or let him suffer? Do you think that your parents could have lived with the fact that their only son had asked them for something that they couldn't do? What of another hunter?

Do you think they would have made his death quick? Painless? Or do you think they would have tied him to the ground to let him fry? You saw what he looked like when he tried to do it himself. Did you want that to happen to him?"

"No. But that's not the point. I killed him." Stephan snorted. "You're a bastard, did you know that?"

"Actually I am, but that's neither here nor there. We're talking about your brother. Answer me, Gab. What would have happened? Or better yet, let's ask your father." Stephan turned to him and stared him right into the eyes. Wiley knew in that moment that he'd have to tell him the truth. There was something powerful compelling him to do so. "Would you have been able to end your son's suffering by cutting his head from his shoulders?"

"No." Wiley knew that even though he'd been made to answer, it really was the truth. He would never have been able to do what Gab did. He looked at her now. "Christ, child, I had no idea how brave you are. Never would I have been able to do...I wouldn't have been able to do anything near what you did."

He stood up and hugged her to him. When she stood near him so stiffly, he thought that he'd been wrong in making her tell him about what had happened. Even if he'd guessed most of it. But she wrapped her arms around him and hugged him back. Wiley felt the tears in his eyes escape and didn't care a fig. His little girl was in his arms, and he was as happy as he could be.

"Dad, I'm so sorry." He felt his heart break for all that she'd been through. "Rusty begged me so hard and he was suffering so much. I couldn't let him. I just couldn't let him suffer any longer."

"Well, of course you couldn't." He pulled back from her but didn't let her go. "And I bet you right now he's smiling down on you."

"Or he's with some girl." He liked that. His son making time with an angel. Wiley laughed with her when she smiled. There was nothing in this world more precious to him than her smile.

"His maker is paying for what he did to him." Wiley looked at Stephan when he spoke. "I've contacted some of the higher ups and they're looking into it. I know it's not much after all you've had to suffer with, but there will be something done. And since he's done it before, there will be plenty done."

"I don't want anyone to lose their job, but he made my son what he was without his permission. What if next time there isn't anyone to help them? What if…what if he takes a child and turns them?" Wiley shivered as he talked to the vampire. "You let me know if I have to testify or anything. I know that Rusty wasn't the greatest kid in the world; hell, truth be known, he was a little on the spoiled side. My fault, my fault entirely…but he was mine, and now because of some hinny hole, he's gone from me and my family. You just let me know."

Stephan grinned and Wiley frowned. When the vampire spoke, there was so much laughter in his voice that Wiley found himself laughing with him. "I don't believe I've ever heard anyone say 'hinny hole' before. But somehow it's not bad coming from you."

"I don't find the need to curse if I don't have to. I can, let me tell you, I can, but not when I'm in mixed company." He nodded toward his daughter, who laughed too. "I'm a good man, but that don't mean I don't get a little riled up. When I do, I use it, but for now I just don't."

Stephan laughed. "I like you, Wiley. You're a great man. I'm going to enjoy getting to know you better too."

They moved off to the kitchen. There they found Jimmy talking to the new cook and a couple of other people. Wiley looked around the room. He was thrilled to death to know that his daughter had done well for herself. He just hoped that she'd be getting more rest now that she'd talked to him about Rusty.

Chapter 15

"The road to hell is paved with people like you." Devon didn't care what the man said. He needed what little powerbase he had. "I'm not very powerful, and yet here you are taking what I have."

"You have enough and that's all that matters." Devon drew back his sword to take the man's head. "You should also know that the Silver Queen will die because of this."

Just as the sword swung forward, the man spoke again. "You mean Gab?" But it was too late to check the swing. Too late for him to find out more than a simple name. And much too late for him to think about what he was doing.

"Mother fuck." Devon watched the head roll back from his shoulders and land three feet away. Picking up the head, he looked into the eyes and screamed at the man. "What do you know? Who is she?"

Of course, nothing was forthcoming. The man was dead, and Devon was still clueless about the girl. As the small, yet much needed, power moved into his body, he realized something else. The man wasn't nearly as powerful as he'd thought. Devon hardly felt the difference in his own power, and he was pissed about that too.

Leaving the man lay where he dropped, Devon made his way back to his hotel. It wasn't a great part of town, and to his way of thinking, another dead body wasn't going to make that much of a stir. As soon as he exited the small, closed-in alley, he saw three vampires go into a building across from him. He followed but at a long distance.

There were four or five more in the smallish building. The three that he'd followed settled on one side of the room, while the rest stayed where they were. Devon didn't think they were friends, but he knew enough about nests to know that you didn't necessarily need to even know the others that slept the day away with you, only that you needed to make sure that they weren't going to kill you when you slept. Devon decided to keep an eye on this place for a few days to see if the bitch showed up. Devon moved to the all-night coffee shop across the street to settle in.

By ten-thirty he was bored out of his mind. The sun had been up for a few hours and other than a few prostitutes that took their *dates* to the side of the building, no one went near it. Devon stood up just as someone sat in the seat across from him. The woman was the most beautiful person he'd ever seen.

"Looking for someone?" He nodded to her question before he could think not to. "Me too. But I think I'm going to have better luck than you are."

"You think so, do you?" She nodded and smiled at him. "And what makes you so sure? You have a crystal ball or something?"

He took an immediate dislike of the woman and lifted his hand off the table to give her a little of his power. Devon knew he could ill afford it, but he wanted to put her in her place. But she slapped her hand over his before he could do anything.

"You do that and I'll have to kill you right now. And what fun would that be?" He felt a chill race down his spine, sweat bead on his forehead and slide down his back. "You're going to sit here and behave yourself or I'm going to have to do just what I said."

"Who are you?" He had a feeling he knew but wanted her to say so. When she stood up, he started to as well when she shook her head. "If you think you can order me around, you're fucking stupid."

"Am I?" A man came from the counter and stood beside her. She glanced at him before looking back at Devon. "This is my good friend, Kaleb. He's new in town and hasn't had a good deal of sleep yet. I wouldn't fuck with him." She headed for the door.

"And why should I care?" The man shifted ever so slightly and Devon felt a burble of a scream escape his mouth. When the man sat down, now a human and no longer part bear, Devon stared at him. "Are you going to kill me?"

"Not today." The waitress came over to take Kaleb's order, and Devon was vaguely aware of how much he'd ordered. It sounded like the entire menu. "He's paying too."

The waitress skipped away, and Devon started to protest about paying for a man's breakfast that had just threatened him. But he stopped when Kaleb lifted his hand and pointed to the window. The woman was entering the building with another man, and Devon knew with certainty who she was.

"The Silver Queen." Kaleb nodded as the waitress brought him a large orange juice and a cup of coffee. "You work for her?"

"Me and a bunch of others. She's good." He poured what Devon thought was a cup of cream into his cup before adding five sugars. "I think maybe she's gathering herself a crew to work faster at taking out the vermin around here. I think you should watch your ass. I believe you're next on her list."

"Me? What have I done to warrant such treatment?" Devon knew that his list was long and colorful, but the man didn't have to know that. But apparently he did. His laughter had heads turning toward them.

"I'd say you should have been taken out today, but she said to wait. I'm thinking she's getting paid for the job across the street and you were messing her up. She called me in to keep an eye on you in the event you got it into your head to go over and try to kill her." Kaleb winked at him as he continued. "Could have been fun, but you'd have made entirely too much noise screaming like a little girl when she killed you, and would have awoken the baby vamps."

She'd been sitting right in front of him and he'd not been able to do a damned thing. And now she had him on her list. When the food arrived for Kaleb, Devon marveled again at the amount. He'd expected the man to simply pick up the plates and eat from them without benefit of silverware, but as Devon watched, he was amazed at the man's manners. He must have said something because he was winked at again.

"My mother would have my butt if I ate like an animal. She used to tell me, 'Kaleb, you are what you eat. And if you eat it like a hog, then that's all you'll ever be.' I think I was chewing on a man's leg at the time." Devon felt his bladder loosen. He wanted to think that Kaleb was kidding about the man's leg, but he wasn't sure.

"What is she going to do to me?" Kaleb looked up at him as he cut through his steak. "I mean, you said I was on her list. Am I to assume she's turning me over to the authorities?"

"You can assume anything you like, I suppose, but that doesn't make it a fact." Kaleb stacked his empty plate on top of the other two he'd emptied. "No, I don't think she has any plans at all to turn you over to anyone. Unless it's the morgue. And that might be iffy too."

"What do you mean by that?" But he was pretty sure he knew. Instead of answering, Kaleb only smiled again. Infuriated, Devon started to stand again. He stopped as soon as four other men in the room stood as well. All of them looked…hungry came to mind, and Devon sat back down. "You can't hold me here."

"You're right, I can't. Go ahead and leave. I'm sure any one of the others in this room would be more than glad to escort you out." Kaleb looked behind him and with a short nod from him, the others sat as well. When he turned back to him, the man looked as relaxed and rested as anyone he'd ever seen. "Would you like to leave now?"

He didn't answer. What would be the point really? Neither of them spoke as Kaleb finished off his meal. When the check was brought, Devon thought about not accepting it, but the look in the other man's eye told him that he wanted him not to take it. Taking it from her, he looked at the total.

"This is over two hundred dollars. Who else did I buy breakfast for?" He pulled out his wallet and took out a credit card. Devon laid it as gently as he could onto the check. Anger surged through him to the point where he wanted to kill. But even he could see that he'd be killed before he drew his next breath.

"You didn't expect me to eat when the rest were sitting there starving, did you?" Devon looked at the men at the counter, who gave him a short wave. "They want you to leave a nice tip too. I'd say about fifty should do it. And in cash."

It was all the cash he had, and he was pretty sure that he knew it. But Devon knew as surely as he was sitting there that refusing would certainly be a mistake. Taking out the cash, he laid it on the table as the waitress returned. Devon was trembling with anger.

"I'm not going to forget this." He signed his name to the bill with a flourish. "I will make you and the rest of them pay before this is through."

"You think so." The woman was suddenly standing next to the table again. "I doubt you make it to the end of the week, Devon Robert Anderson, much less make plans to take me and my crew out."

She sat down when Kaleb stood up. All he could think about was that she knew his name. All of it. When she smiled at him, he felt his body freeze in fear. Devon wondered for a second if these were his last moments on earth.

"No, they're not." He looked at her sharply. "Yeah, I can read your mind. Fucking lot of shit up there, but I can read it. So can the man sitting at the counter and the woman over there. I'm going to give you something that I doubt very much you'll take."

"What is it? And just for the record, I can read your mind as well." She only threw back her head and laughed. She knew that he was full of shit. "Why did you kill Valda?"

"She tried to kill me. And I took exception to that. As for what I plan to do with you, well, that's going to be up to you. At least for now. I'm going to give you one chance and only one before I set up the means to kill you. Are you willing to listen?" He nodded, not sure what she was offering, but he thought he might take her up on it. With a sad shake to her head, he knew she didn't believe any more than he did that she wasn't going to have to kill him. If she could.

"I have a question first." She nodded. "What did you do with all her power? You don't seem to be all that strong from it. Or did it just fade out because she wasn't fully aware of what she had?"

She lifted her hand and wiggled her fingers. Devon watched as the air around them stirred and small flickers of lightning started to form. When one of them arched off and touched his hand, he screamed. He felt it all the way to the balls of his feet.

"I have it all. Something you should think about if you decided not to take me up on my offer." He nodded, too afraid not to. "You're going to stop using magic all together."

"I will not." Devon put his hand over his mouth as soon as the words spilled from him. "I can't. I'll die."

"That's sort of the point. If you don't stop, and I mean as of this very second, the next time you see me I'm going to take your head." As soon as the words left her mouth, she disappeared.

Devon looked around the restaurant and saw that everyone was gone that had been sitting at the counter. The waitress came over to take the empty plates away or he would have assumed that he'd dreamed the whole thing up. Standing on unsteady feet, Devon staggered to the door and out to his car. The sun was setting again. Looking at his watch, he realized that several hours had gone by, almost nine. Sitting in his car, he leaned his head back on the seat and tried to think. As soon as he closed his eyes, he could see her there. The Silver Queen was laughing at him.

~~~

Gab paced a few more times before she tried to sit again. Jimmy didn't say anything to her, though he wanted to grab her and tell her to stop. She was on edge, and he wondered how long it would take before she exploded.

"He won't stop, will he?" Jimmy didn't have to ask her what she was talking about. Devon was all she'd spoken of since they'd broken the connection with him over an hour ago. "The witch said that he'd run. I don't think that's going to happen."

"I don't either. From what I've heard, he pretty much thinks he's the shit." He smiled when she snorted. "Not my words but those of the witch. She said he was a fool if he thought you couldn't beat him."

"I don't know if I can. I can use a few parlor tricks but nothing on the scale she said it was in." Jimmy had heard some of the things that Devon could do, and he, too, was blown away. The man could bring someone back from the dead.

"You'll do it. She said you have all that stuff that Valda had. You're just going to have to learn to use it." She looked at him as if he had three heads. He sort of felt that way right now. Because, for as much power as she had, he did too.

"Did I tell you what happened to me when I was in the kitchen last night?" She stopped pacing to stare at him. So he nodded and told her how stupid he'd felt. "I was reaching for a glass when Milford came in behind me. I had heard him, but I didn't realize he was that close. When he asked me if he could help me, I handed him the glass. I guess our fingers brushed or something, because he ended up across the room on the floor. I'm pretty sure he's going to want a raise after this."

Gab laughed. It was what he'd hoped for and he told her how Nova, Milford's wife, said that she wanted some of their juice as well. Pulling her to him, he held her. That's when he looked around the room.

"When did we get new furniture in here?" She laughed again. "I swear this room had two couches and two chairs when we came in here this morning."

"I asked the same thing. The witch said it was the faeries. They like changing things around until they get it the way we seem to relax in here. I guess we should expect it in all the rooms until we're comfortable. I've told them to leave the bedroom where it is. I love that room." He did as well and told her so. "I like the colors in here. It's very warm."

It was too. Browns and golds were the most dominate colors, but there were deep reds and blues as well. And the furniture appealed to him better. Instead of the couches, there were several overstuffed chairs with ottomans. Three love seats instead of chairs graced either side of the fireplace. And the mantel now held pictures of outdoor scenes instead of art deco. When Gab snuggled into his throat, however, he forgot about the room and anything in it.

"I want you." He moved her across his lap so that she faced him, her legs on either side of his. He wanted her too.

"Do you have any attachment to these clothes?" She shook her head but put her hand over his when he reached down to tear them off her.

"You can do this." Moving her hand down his chest, his shirt disappeared. As soon as her hand touched the front of his pants, he was naked and throbbing in her hand. His cock thickened as she stroked him. "I want to taste you."

Without waiting for him to say anything, she scooted off him and down to the floor. When she spread his legs and moved between them, he cupped his hands over her shoulders and willed her clothing away as well. Christ, he was looking at a goddess.

"I won't last long." She smiled at him and licked his crown. "Christ, if you do that again I'm going to come. It's been a while."

"We had sex this morning." He moaned when she licked him again. "And this afternoon. And an hour ago. You're going to break something if we keep that up."

"I don't care." Jimmy curled his hand into her hair. "Take me, Gab, please? I need to feel your mouth over—"

She swallowed him. Jimmy knew he was more than likely hurting her, but he couldn't seem to stop. Moving his hips up and down, he fucked her mouth hard. When she cupped his balls, he felt his world spin and his climax race over him. As soon as she gave his balls a little twist, he came, shouting out her name. But it wasn't enough. He had to have her.

"Stand up." Glaze-eyed, she did as he commanded her. When she was standing before him, all he could think about was tasting her, and he leaned forward, buried his mouth over her, and nipped. She was soaking wet, and her clit was as hard as he was. Lapping at her as fast as he could, he still missed a lot of her cream. Growling, he pulled her around and tossed her to the couch. He settled between her thighs as she'd done to him.

"My turn." Lifting her legs so that they were over his shoulders, he leaned forward again and suckled on her clit. Lifting his head, he looked at her. "When I've had my fill, I'm going to have you. I want you to stand behind this couch and hang on. I want to fuck you from behind until you scream."

Her nod turned to a scream when he took her clit into his mouth again. Jimmy drank from her greedily, and every time she came, he felt his wolf want more. Letting a little of his beast go, he let him drink from her and heard Gab scream over and over her release. Jimmy growled at her to stand now.

Watching her move into the position he wanted, he fisted his cock. He'd never been so hard in all his life and wasn't sure how long he was going to last, even after coming down her throat not ten minutes ago. Standing up and moving behind her, he felt his wolf snarl at him to take her. Jimmy held his cock as he rubbed the tip in her juices.

"Jimmy, please. I need you." He teased her with his cock, and she rocked back to take more of him in. "Please, damn it, take me."

He slammed forward and into her. Her scream had him leaning over her and wrapping his arm around her. Jimmy was sure he'd not hurt her, but he knew that if he moved now, it would be over before it started. And as much as he wanted to fill her with his seed, he wanted this to last too.

"I'm going to mark you again." She moaned, and he licked her shoulder. "As soon as I can move without coming."

Her giggle gave him the much needed pause. When he moved slowly inside of her, he felt her muscles ripple around him, hugging him tightly. Reaching her breasts, he cupped them in his palms and twisted her nipples with his thumb and finger.

"You're so tight around me." He licked her shoulder again before continuing. "I want to fill you with our child soon. I'd love to see you swollen with a baby and watch it move beneath your skin."

"Jimmy, please." He smiled when she slid her hand over his, then down to her pussy. "If you don't help me, then I will."

Jimmy pressed his hand over hers and felt her heat. Sliding their fingers into her, she moaned again. He felt his climax start to move over him and knew that he wasn't going to be long behind her when she came. Nuzzling her neck, he scraped his teeth over her flesh. And when she cried out, he sank his teeth deep into her. Jimmy felt his beast rise up, and before he could stop it, he tore hard at her. When she screamed again, he knew that he'd hurt her but could do nothing about it. He threw back his head and howled out his own release.

Jimmy dropped his head on her back and laid there. He couldn't move, and was sure if the house were invaded he'd be dead. When Gab shifted slightly on her feet, he tried to work up the energy to move off her knowing that he was hurting her, but he couldn't do it. Laughing, he kissed her back.

"You'll have to carry me, I'm afraid. You've killed me." She giggled again, and he found that he loved the sound as much as he did hearing her say she loved him. "Do you think we could stay this way for the next few hours?"

"I think the staff will be embarrassed." She shifted again. "How about you take us to the bedroom?

It works just like our clothing thing did. Just will us there."

Thinking about the bedroom and them there, he found himself lying flat on his back in the middle of their bed and Gab next to him. Pulling her to him, he reached over and pulled the comforter over them and closed his eyes. Tomorrow, he decided, he was going to learn all these neat tricks.

Chapter 16

Devon had a plan. And looking over it again, he decided it was a great plan. Even better than the one he'd had concerning Valda. This one was foolproof. And if he did say so himself, it was brilliant.

Now all he had to do was get the girl to come to him. And he was pretty sure he had the perfect way to get that done as well. Just use any one of the men who'd been with her that day. As soon as he figured out where to find them, he was going to finish the bitch.

"I've got feelers out for those men you talked about. And so you know, we're not fucking with that bear. Did you know that he's a brown grizzly? I don't fuck with them." Jennings sat down as he continued. "And he weighs a good deal more than an average grizzly, even for a shifter. I would say close to a ton and none of it's fat either. Motherfucker is huge."

"I'm well aware of how large he is. As I've said to you several times, I've met him. And there are any number of others that I told you about." Jennings nodded. "Well, have you had any luck in finding them?"

"Nope. Do you have any idea how many shifters are in this area? I mean the real number? I would have guessed fifty or so. But I'd be wrong. There are over three thousand of them. And looking for a tall man with dark hair that may or may not shift into a wolf doesn't really help any. Perhaps if you'd of gotten a name? Or a picture I might have better luck." He snorted as he continued. "It's like hunting for an Irishman with red hair in Ireland. It's not happening."

"I want one of them found. Today." When Jennings stood up, Devon took a step back. This was becoming a bad habit with him. He was sick to death of being afraid all the time. But he had the stellation set up and now the moons were right. And the bitch wasn't any closer to coming to him than he was finding her. "I need her by midnight tomorrow. If you don't find her, then all bets are off. You're going to be on my list."

"Like I give two fucks about your list." Jennings took a menacing step toward him again, and Devon backed up quickly. Laughing, Jennings left the room, shaking his head. Devon decided that he was going to kill the man first thing after this was over.

He was losing power. Not having anyone to replenish it was hurting him as well. In two days he stood to have the greatest power of all time, and he could barely leave his room for fear of using some of what he had left. Looking in the mirror, he could see the effects of losing what little he had.

His face was sagging, and dark spots were appearing more and more all over his cheeks and lips. Gray hair now replaced the dark hair he'd had three days ago. And his hands looked like someone had splattered them with brown paint. Not to mention he was hurting more than he'd ever hurt before. If no help came to him soon, he'd die, and not just die, but shrivel up into a dust ball and scatter in the winds dead.

The knock at his door had him sitting down. He'd been a vain man before and now that he had reason to hide he did so with a vengeance. When he bid the person enter, he nearly told the man to leave again when he stood looking at him as if he'd never seen him before. He snapped at the man to say whatever it was he had to say.

"There is a young man here to see you, sire. He said that he has word about the Queen. He mentioned a reward." Devon told him to let the man come in. And before he could straighten his desk up, the man was standing there.

"She said I was to come and see you." Devon stilled in waving a chair to the man. "The Queen, she said I was to come and see you. I have a message from her."

"What...?" He had to clear his throat his had gone bone dry. "What did she have to say to me?"

The young man held out an envelope and Devon stared at it. He knew better than to take it. It more than likely had all kinds of spells on it that would make him do whatever it was she commanded him to do. Or a spell that would kill him. He looked at the young man.

"Read it to me." The guy grinned as if he'd expected him to tell him that. Devon almost snatched it from him to read it himself but waited while he slowly opened it. By the time he finally pulled the sheet of paper from the insides, Devon was ready to kill the man.

"Devon Robert Anderson. You are hereby ordered to cease and desist in all activities in hunting for someone to bring me to you. If you want to meet, then just tell me where, you dick-faced moron." The young man looked up, grinning. "I'd say she doesn't like you much. What did you do to piss her off?"

"None of your business. Finish the damned letter." He shrugged and continued with a phone number and email address. It was his choice on which way he was to contact her.

Devon waited for an hour to call her. It wasn't that he was trying to make a point, but it took him that long to build up the nerve. She was powerful, and Devon had a feeling that she might know just how much she'd gained by killing Valda.

"You're not going to kill me, you know that, right?" she said in way of greeting. "I'm only meeting you to kill you, fucking ass. I told you to stop, but did you listen? Nope. And now you have to pay."

"And what makes you think I won't kill you?" She snorted, a nasty habit he'd just learned about from others. "I can, you know. I'm very powerful, and can take you out without so much as lifting my fingers."

"Whatever. Meet me in the center of your stellation at midnight tomorrow night and we'll see who wears the big boy panties." He didn't understand what she was saying, but before he could ask her what the fuck she meant, she continued. "That is the right time, isn't it? All your moons will be in alignment, and whatever else you need to make this shit work."

"It is. But you have to come alone." She snorted again. "And will you please stop with that shit? You're giving me a headache in the worst way. Just be there. Since I guess you know where it is I won't bother with asking you if you need directions. And, as I said, come alone."

"Not going to happen. I have a mate, and he comes where I do." A mate? Devon tried to think what that meant. Even if he killed her, he'd have to die too. They would share the magic. Mother fuck balls. This was getting harder and harder to finish.

"Bring him then. I could care less." Devon was already making plans to kill them both even as he put the phone in the cradle. Killing them both would be the only way for him to get the magic he needed, and even then it was a long shot. Gathering up all the things he needed, he went to the garage. It was time to call in help. And by help he knew that the only way to defeat this woman was to bring her worst enemy. Vampires would want her dead anyway.

"What do you want?" Devon nearly wet himself when the vampire showed up so quickly. Looking down at the spell he'd used, it said it may take up to an hour or more. And not to be surprised if the new moon had to be involved.

The man standing before him didn't look like a vamp he'd ever seen. In fact he looked like a regular human. "Well?"

"I would like for you to help me kill the Silver Queen." The man nodded and Devon continued with his needs. "She has killed a great many of your kind and I wish to help you rid the world of her kind."

"And take her power too." Devon tried to look affronted, but he knew he didn't pull it off when the man laughed. "I'm a great deal older than you are, and I know a sorry-assed mage when I see one. What is it you want from me?"

"Your help in the way of security. I wish for you to give me some of your men to hold her and her mate down while I kill them." The vampire sat down, and that's when Devon knew that he wasn't in the room with him but on some other plane. "I have the spells ready and a stellation ready to go. I would like for you to help me."

"And what do I get out of this? Fame for killing the Silver Queen? I think not. I understand that she works for some pretty powerful people." Devon didn't know that but it mattered little. As soon as she was dead he'd be the most powerful being. "What time and I'll think about having a few of my men there."

"Eleven-thirty. The plan is to take her at midnight, and once she is gone, I will share the wealth by giving you her mate." Devon knew that he'd have to kill the mate too or nothing would come to him, but the vampire didn't have to know that. "I will make sure that any rewards that are on her head are yours as well."

Devon went back to his house after cleaning up his spell. He'd never had one work so well before and was smiling when he entered the house. Just thirty-one more hours and he'd have her magic. He decided to lie down and nap for a bit. Devon wanted to be at his best when things went down.

~~~

Gab didn't know what to say. Stephan had talked with the mage and now they were going to help her. She looked at Jimmy when he took her hand.

"This is going to work. Stephan said that his men will be there now to protect us instead of hiding in the darkness." She nodded, thinking of all the things that could and would go wrong if Devon figured it out.

"He'll hurt them." Stephan laughed, as did Samuel. She wondered, not for the first time, how he'd known to come there. Gab glanced over at Kaleb. "What do you think of this?"

"I don't have to get my hands dirty, and I get to play with vamps. Sounds like a good deal to me. Maybe I can get lucky with one of them females. I hear they like it rough." Kaleb winked at her. "Maybe we can get a little boxing in too if you're up for it afterwards."

Kaleb had found her in the workout room that had appeared yesterday morning. She had been thinking about finding a gym in town while she'd been standing in front of a door that led to an empty room. She and Jimmy had been opening doors every day to see what other things the faeries had changed. The room had surprised her. Not just in size but the amount of equipment in it. The boxing bag had been her first exercise.

"I don't want to have to hurt you. Sorry." Kaleb laughed, and she joined him. "I guess we can have a round or two, but it really will have to be after this other crap is over. I sort of have a full plate right now."

"I would say so." She looked at Samuel when he spoke. "I need for you to do something for me. After this is over. I want you to go with Kennedy to do some shopping."

She was already shaking her head no. "I will not go shopping with your wife. I'm not an idiot. Her idea of shopping is to try on everything she touches and then not buy a damned thing. I don't have time or the energy for that shit."

"Please?" She wanted to smack the man, and when he batted his eyes at her, she did slap him. "You would do me a huge favor and I'd owe you."

That sounded good. Before she could ask him how much he'd owe her, Milford stepped into the room. He did not look happy when he announced dinner.

"What's up your butt?" He nearly laughed and she knew it. "Your wife trying to get you to tie her to the bed again? Shame on you, Milford. You should try new things."

"No, my lady, it's not that. It's the faeries again. They've expanded the pantry and added things that…well, frankly, I'm not sure what to do with." He flushed, and she smiled. "There are things in there that I would just as soon not know for sure what they are."

Now she had to see. Going to the kitchen with him, she could see that they'd been working in this room as well. The refrigerator was twice the size as the day before and the windows had been expanded as well. There was a view out them that took her breath away. She looked at the door that he'd been talking about.

There were the usual things in the first three shelves. Going to where Milford had indicated she could see that they had expanded the room. It was nearly twice the size as it had been before. And the shelves were already bulging at the seams. She picked up the first item and nearly dropped it when she read the label.

"What do you suppose they think you're going to cook that uses lizard hearts?" She put the jar back on the shelf and turned to him. But he was gone and in his place was the witch. "You want to explain this to me?"

"They think that when you defeat the mage you'll be using these things. I shall tell them you'll need training first." The witch smiled at her. "It is time to tell you my name."

"Why?' Gab didn't think she wanted her name and told her so. "I think I like things just the way they are, thanks.

I'm pretty sure knowing your name will get me into all sorts of trouble that I would just as soon not have to deal with."

"It's Calypso. As in Homer's Odyssey. I was named for the sea nymph who kept Odysseus on her island for seven years." They moved into the kitchen where it too was empty of people. "I should like for you to use it to summon me when you need help."

"You think I'm going to need help?" Calypso shrugged. "You know that's not at all helpful. Either I will or I won't. Which is it?"

"You will and you won't." Gab growled at her. "I'm sorry, but I do not know if you will need me or not. But I should like for you to be able to summon me if you do. And you having my name will help you."

"But I thought that I had to have your whole name." Calypso said nothing. "Are you telling me that this is your whole name? That no one gave you a sire name?"

"I was born in a place where names were all you needed. And first names were all that anyone would use. So to save time, we did away with such things as surnames. Besides, who cares where you were born from so long as you're a person of respect and worth? And you are." Calypso sat down as she continued. "I should also like to know what your plans are for the meeting with Devon. By the way, he is not expecting the vampires to turn on him. He believes them to be fully under the control of Stephan."

"He told me." Gab started to pace the kitchen. She thought better that way. "I have a plan. It's to kill him. I've given him fair warning, as you've said I had to, and now he has to go. What I don't understand is why you haven't done it on your own. It's not like you don't have the power to do so."

"I do, but in killing him I'd get what he has. I have no wish for any more power. Besides, after this is finished, you will owe me a boon. I will want you to carry it out as quickly as possible." Gab had figured out what Calypso had wanted from her. She wanted to die, and she wanted Gab to do it.

"Why me?" Calypso smiled. "And if you think that's comforting, then you're wrong. I just want to know why you think I should be the one to end your life. You have to have a reason, and you need to tell me."

"I can give you many, but the main one is because I wish for you to have what I am." Gab shook her head but didn't get the chance to say anything, like *no fucking way.* "And you will do so quickly without fanfare."

"And you think that Stephan won't?" She nodded, then shook her head. "I don't understand you. You give me your name to summon you. Then you ask me to kill you off. How the hell is your name going to be useful if you're dead?"

"It will be a way to summon me from beyond, and you will be surprised how much information I can give you from there." Calypso smiled again. This time it was a sad looking one. "You will understand once this business with Devon Robert Anderson is taken care of. You'll see."

Gab was still sitting at the table when Jimmy came in. He looked worried, and she could understand. She was worried too. When he asked her if she was coming to eat, she told him she was and stood up. Before she could take a step, Samuel came into the room.

"I'm so sorry." She knew as soon as he spoke that something had happened. "I have a car coming now to take you to the hospital. I swear to you he's going to get the best care possible."

"My dad." Samuel nodded, and she felt her world start to tumble. "What happened? My mom? Where is she?"

"With him. The medic said he thought he had a heart attack. They're taking him to surgery right now to see. I've called in every favor I can find and they're going to make sure he's going to make it." She followed them to the front of the house where Nova stood waiting for her. She took the coat from the older woman, and the hug. Gab felt numb.

"I need to call Stephan. If he can help him, I'd like for him to be there." No one answered her, but she didn't care. He'd help her with her dad or she'd kick his ass. "And don't forget to call your wife. I'm sure she'll be worried too."

Before she could think about anything else, they were standing in the emergency room. Gab looked at Jimmy, who kissed her and smiled. "I've been practicing," was all he said, and she knew that he'd taken her there. Moving down the hall, she tried to think of something to say to her mom, who stood in the hall.

The hug they exchanged was tight, and Gab didn't want to let her go. She knew that her dad had a bad heart, and when she'd found that he'd gone back to work, she'd thrown a fit. But it had happened while he'd been with her, and now he was hurting.

"We were going in the restaurant when he suddenly clutched his chest. He tried to tell me it was nothing. Then he fell over. I wanted to smack him." Gab nodded at her mom. "The old poop said he'd live forever now that you were happy."

"He will. I'm going to make sure of it." She sat with her mom to wait. The surgery was supposed to last about three hours. In six she had to be at the stellation. Her life had just gotten crazy again.

"Mrs. Parker?" They both looked up when the doctor spoke. He looked grim, and Gab had the sudden urge to tell him to get the fuck away. "Your husband is going to be a bit longer than we thought. He has a great deal of blockage, and some of his arteries are clogged and need to be cleaned. He is—"

"I want to see him." He started shaking his head when she spoke. "You didn't understand me. I said I want to see him, I wasn't asking you for permission. Where is he?"

"I'm sorry, miss, but I can't allow that. As his doctor, I can only—" She lifted him off the floor and held him there while he struggled. Samuel said her name twice before she looked at him.

"I want to see my dad." Samuel nodded and asked her to put the nice man down. "I will when he tells me where he is."

"Gab, this isn't helping. Honey, let the man go." She looked at her mom and felt her heart break. "Please, baby, let the doctor go."

Gab dropped him. Her body was still humming with power and she looked at Jimmy. He seemed to understand and asked the doctor where her father was. He told them he was in the operating room. She moved down the hall toward room three. Before she got there, two security officers blocked her way.

"I will kill you if you fuck with me." She pulled out the blade at her side. "I have a gun, too, that I'm not afraid to use on you. Now move."

They parted ways as soon as she felt someone come up behind her. Without turning, she knew it was Samuel. Walking to the operating room, she looked at the nurses prepping her dad. After ordering them out, she went to his bed to see that he'd been hooked up to monitors and other things. She asked Samuel to help her.

"Jimmy is watching the door. He said to give you whatever you need." He looked around the empty room, save the two of them and her dad. "Are we going to operate on him?"

"No. I have a feeling I can help him all by myself." He nodded and asked her what if she couldn't. "Then I guess I've just killed him."

Walking to him slowly, Gab felt the power race to her fingertips. She had to touch him, but was almost afraid to. Reaching for Calypso, she asked her for her help.

"Touch him, child. You know that you can." She nodded once and reached out to touch her dad. As soon as she did, the monitors started to scream at them and her dad's heart

rate picked up speed. When he screamed, she knew for sure that she'd killed him.

Chapter 17

Everything was ready. All the vampires were in place, and there were an untold number of other beings around the perimeter just waiting for the signal. Kennedy looked at her mate and reached for his hand. This was show time and she'd never been so afraid in her life.

"Ye think she'll be able to *bhuachan*...win, I mean? There be a great many here, but whose side do ye think they be on?" Samuel squeezed her hand in answer. "Aye, you are a sap, aren't ye?"

"I am. And you as well. Don't think I can't see your tears. You're worried for them too." She nodded, unable to speak for a moment. "I have grown fond of the girl despite her being a pain in the ass. And Jimmy loves her."

He did too. Any fool could see that. When a man suddenly appeared in the center of the large open area, she watched. Kennedy supposed that she might have had a better view from the trees, but Gab had asked her not to do that. She had told her that she wasn't sure what was going to happen, and having the forest catch fire was a possibility. Kennedy told her that she'd wait there.

"I've been thinking." She smiled at Samuel, waiting for him to say something smart about her thinking being dangerous. "You should hire her to be your enforcer too. I understand from Jimmy that they be not taking the job that Stephan asked them to."

"I heard too. Jimmy said he wants to teach. I would never have guessed it, but he said he has a hankering to be a science teacher." Samuel nodded toward the field. "It looks like it's about to begin."

"So you came. Good for you. Now what the fuck do you want?" Kennedy had to smile. Gab was nothing if not direct. "I'm a little busy to be fucking around tonight, so say whatever it is you want and let me kill you."

"I think that's not going to happen. In fact, you should know that I plan to kill you." Devon's laughter rang across the field. "And then I'm going to kill your mate."

"Fat chance. What did you do, kill another mage to get a little more juice? You're going to need it before we finish here, I think." Gab stretched her arms up over her head, and sparks shot from her fingertips. "You see, I've been playing around with this shit, and I think I can take you."

"You should look around, my dear. I've been playing too." The field was filled with vampires. Most of them worked with Kennedy and Samuel, but a few of them—well, most of them—were subjects to Stephan. The few who weren't were there to pledge to him afterwards. Kennedy just hoped there was an afterwards.

"Vampires? What happened to us coming alone? You didn't do what you said you were going to do, and that makes whatever I do to you fair game." Devon laughed. "You think this is funny? I'm so over this shit."

The arch of light jumped from her fingers to Devon. He didn't move. Kennedy wasn't sure if it was because it had happened so fast or the fact that he didn't believe she could harm him. The ground burned right in front of him.

"Impressive. Not strong, but a nice, pretty light show." Devon lifted his hands, and the vampires moved as one toward her, and in the front of the line was Stephan. He looked very regal, Kennedy thought. Gab turned in a circle, seemingly taking in the beings around her.

"Nice. Did you have to sell your soul to have them here?" She looked back at Devon when he didn't answer her. "You should probably know something. I hate to break it to you, but I kinda knew they were coming and brought in a few of my own men to help out."

The field was filled with the rest of the hidden beings. Most of them had shifted and stood circling around the vamps as if to attack. Instead of moving toward them, they sat in the circle and waited. A lone wolf came forward and stood beside her, and Stephan moved to her other side.

"You know them?" Stephan nodded. "And you knew this woman even before I asked you to come to stand with me?"

"Of course. She works for me. For all of us actually. She's the Silver Queen and takes out rogues. Rogues that would have humans hunting us, people burning our homes simply because of who we are, what we are. You would have her die to fulfill your own plan. Mine is to live in peace." Stephan raised his hand, and the vampires took a step forward. "I commanded them, and if I had my way, I'd let them have you."

"But?" Kennedy caught her laugher before it spilled out. He actually had to ask? Didn't he know that she was going to kill him and end this? More than likely he thought himself above such petty things as following the rules.

"By order of the Council of Vampires, the House of Magick, and the rest of the beings that you've managed to piss off for years, I hereby sentence you to death. And as I have been appointed to do such, I ask you now, what kind of death do you want?"

"I'm sorry?" Kennedy found herself leaning forward to find out what she'd meant too. Devon asked her again and Gab shrugged.

"Quick and painless? Slow and painful? Or do you prefer the one where I get to choose? I so hope you go for that one. I'm sure you'll not enjoy it as much as I do." Gab took a step forward, and Devon rose off the ground. "Choose."

"You're insane. I didn't come here to die. I came here to kill you. This is not the way things are supposed to go. Let me down and let's start over." Devon looked like he was serious, and Kennedy did laugh then. The man was nuts.

"You think I should let you kill me because that was your plan?" Devon nodded at her. Gab laughed and looked around. "Do you think I should let him have a do over?"

"I think you should simply get this over with." She nodded at Jimmy and turned back to Devon, and before she could figure out what her plan was, Devon's head was rolling across the ground toward her. But it was far from over. As soon as Kennedy started forward, she was blown back. The explosion was so loud she was sure she'd never hear again. As her head hit the ground, she wondered briefly if someone had caught her, but she was out before that thought fully formed.

~~~

"I most certainly did not." Jimmy had to hold onto his laughter or Gab might turn on him. Right now she was tearing a new ass into Samuel, and Jimmy was enjoying the show. Samuel looked at him before looking back at Gab as he continued. "I most certainly did not have a medic on standby. All I asked for them to be was nearby, not right here."

"And how is that not on standby? You moronic dick, I told you I had this under control. What if one of those ambulances had gotten caught in the cross fire and a tank of oxygen blew up? Then what would have happened to your family?" Jimmy wanted to point out that one had indeed been in the blast, but held his tongue when Samuel spoke. It was sort of fun watching his best friend get his ass handed to him.

"I've asked you three times to stop calling me names. I know that you're upset, but name calling is just childish."

When she growled low, Samuel crossed his arms over his chest and glared. "And that is uncalled for as well. I'm only trying to figure out what to tell the council. They keep asking me what happened. And other than you taking off his fucking head, I don't know what happened."

"Isn't that enough?" Gab started pacing again and Jimmy watched her. He knew what had happened, and they had decided that with the help of Calypso no one would know that the two of them had gotten the power. Nor would they know that in the time that everyone was knocked out, Gab had killed the witch as well. It was just what they'd known she'd want for her help.

"I don't think they're buying that you beheaded him and he disappeared." Samuel looked like he wanted to ask more, but turned away from her instead. "And the witch is missing. Stephan said that she's gone. I'm not sure what that means either."

"It means that you should leave it the fuck alone." Samuel turned back to Gab when she spoke. "I mean it. You should just walk away and tell them the truth. You don't know what happened, and you have no idea what happened to the body."

"Do you?" She didn't answer him. Samuel looked at Jimmy with a raised brow, but he said nothing more. Turning instead, he moved to the door. "I'm going to let it go. So long as nothing comes back to bite me in the ass. And when it does, don't be surprised to find that I've thrown you under the fucking bus."

As the door closed behind him, Jimmy looked at Gab. She looked exhausted. He supposed it was the long nights at the hospital and now this meeting with Samuel. But her dad was coming home tomorrow, so he was hoping that she'd get some rest then. He pulled her into his arms.

"I went to the stellation today. The grass is starting to turn green again." It had been a burnt area all within the inner area of the two stars. "I think there might be some growth in there by mid-summer next year."

"Calypso said that I returning her to the earth would make it so the black magic wouldn't taint the area so badly." She looked up at him as she continued. "I hope I did the right thing in killing her. She was so desperate to be let go."

"You did just what she wanted. And I think that will be what keeps us sane." He shivered when he thought of the aftermath of the explosion. "They should have all been killed. Everyone there should have died."

"But they didn't. We saved them." He walked with her beside him to the living room. Once again, it had been changed around. She smiled when she sat in the large round chair that he knew hadn't been around since the early seventies.

"I think I would like to talk to someone about the faeries. I think that they should have a single room they can play in but leave the rest of the house to us." She shook her head, and he groaned. "You like all of this changing crap?"

"Actually, I do. And I've talked to them about the bedroom. Plus, there will be no more changing the rooms while we have company." He laughed when she mentioned the time they'd moved the entire living room around while Samuel and Kennedy had been over. "I can still see Samuel's face. He looked like he was going to have a kitten."

"Your parents don't seem to mind it too much." She shook her head. "And Milford and Nova are fine with it now so long as they leave the pantry alone. No adding things that aren't for us to eat."

"And they aren't to mess with the dishwasher either. Did I tell you that one of the brownies was locked inside it during a cycle? They think it's a ride now. I had to put my foot down about that one too." She laughed. "Of course, we have to let them inside on their birthday. As a sort of treat."

"Of course." He sat in the chair opposite to her and smiled. His life had become surreal, and he loved it very much. "Now, we need to talk about the pool house. Did you know that we're now the first aide center for the forest? Yesterday, I walked in on a tree nymph giving birth. Not anything I want to see again."

"I hear you there." As they settled into their night, Jimmy thought of his friends who didn't have mates, and wondered what was in store for them. He also thought about Stephan trying to find a replacement for the two of them. He wished him all the luck.

About the Author

Kathi Barton, author of the bestselling series Force of Nature, lives in Nashport, Ohio with her husband Paul. In addition to writing full time Kathi likes to spend time with her eight grandkids, three children and three children-in-laws. She writes to relax and have fun.

Her muse, a cross between Jimmy Stewart and Hugh Jackman brings them to life for her readers in a way that has them coming back time and again for more. Her favorite genre is paranormal romance with a great deal of spice. You can visit Kathi on line and drop her an email if you'd like. She loves hearing from her fans. aaronskiss@gmail.com.

Follow Kathi on her blog:
http://kathisbartonauthor.blogspot.com/

www.ingramcontent.com/pod-product-compliance
Lightning Source LLC
Chambersburg PA
CBHW032127170626
46808CB00006B/2137